Two Weeks In Corfu

By Ruth Barringham

Published by

Cheriton House Publishing

Queensland

Australia

ISBN: 978-0-6484395-0-9

An Adult Romance Story

This is a work of fiction including the story and the characters. Any likeness to any person living or dead is purely coincidental.

Two Weeks In Corfu

Chapter 1 - Friday Evening

"Damn it!" Muttered Sofia as she clicked the switch several more times.

She was tired, in need of a shower, hungry, but her hotel room had no electricity.

She wheeled her suitcase into the dark room beyond the open door, walked back outside, closed the door and went back to the reception to complain.

The man at the reception desk seemed unsympathetic and told her that he would send someone as soon as possible.

Sofia returned to her room. It was a pleasant walk back along the winding path that curved it's way through the sprawling gardens and passed many other rooms.

It had been 7.30pm when she arrived at her room here at Ionia Bianco in Corfu. This would be her vacation home for the next two weeks.

The rooms were more like studio apartments because they had a small kitchen as well as a bathroom. The family rooms also had a separate bedroom with twin beds.

All the rooms were set out like cabins with up to three in a row, and each had a separate patio at the back.

It was late September so it wasn't as busy as it would have been in summer, but the weather was still warm, or at least warmer than back in England now.

Her journey here had begun at 7.30 am when a taxi had arrived at her house in Bath and driven her to the train station.

From there she caught a train to Heathrow Airport for a 10.30 direct flight.

Once she arrived in Corfu, she put her watch forward two hours to local time and caught the bus to her hotel. The bus was organised by the travel company and so was dropping people at other resorts and hotels along the way. Sofia's resort was the last drop off so it had taken two hours to get here.

Then after a long, crowded wait at the reception, she'd arrived at her room only to find the lights weren't working. In fact there seemed to be no electricity working in her room at all.

She opened the door into the darkness once more and then sat on the doorstep to wait.

Her room was the end one of three. There was another room on her left and another one after that. A path ran in front of all three and continued on past her room and joined the longer path that meandered through all the grounds, which were lit at night, unlike Sofia's room.

As she looked at the main pathway to her right, she heard footsteps coming towards her from the left.

She turned to see who it was, hoping it was someone coming to fix her electric problem.

It was the dirty blonde guy, smiling at her as he approached.

"Waiting for someone?" he asked cheerfully.

"Yeah, someone with electricity for my room." She told him.

"Come to the bar and have a drink. There are plenty of lights there."

"I just want my own lights so that I can unpack.

"Maybe I'll see you later then." And with that he carried on walking to the main path and disappeared out of sight around the corner.

He seemed pleasant enough. She'd nicknamed him "the dirty blonde guy" because she didn't know his name or anything about him, but she had run into him repeatedly throughout the journey of getting here, and even though he was a stranger it was comforting to see a familiar face when she was so far away from home in a foreign country where she'd never been before.

She'd first encountered the dirty blonde guy at Heathrow airport while queuing at the boarding gate. She didn't know he was standing behind her until he said "Excuse me."

That was when she turned around and saw him for the first time.

He was roughly her age, around 30, slim, fair skinned, fair haired and seemed to have a permanent smile on his face. His hair, although fair, was not blonde. But neither was it brunette. It was more of a dirty blonde colour and hung in waves to just above his shoulders.

"Are you only £2.99?" he asked her, his smile never fading.

She wasn't sure how to respond and wondered at that moment if he was crazy.

He put his hand up to her long dark hair and pulled slightly. She felt something come away.

He held up his hand to show a fluorescent orange price sticker that was now stuck to his finger.

Sofia had been browsing at an airport book store while waiting for her flight and some of the books did have those sticky fluorescent price tickets on them. She must have accidentally got too close to the shelves and got it stuck to her hair.

The dirty blonde guy joked, "You'd better not wear this if you don't want people to know you're cheap."

Sofia gave a small laugh, peeled the ticket from his fingers, screwed it up and threw it on the floor.

She couldn't think of an appropriate and witty response so she simply said "Thanks" and turned around again.

Once on board she tried to find her seat which was about half way down the plane.

Further ahead of her were three young guys standing up, who were all acting pretty drunk.

As she approached them, they all turned to look at her. Two of them continued trying to stow their onboard luggage in the overhead compartments while the one closest to her smiled leerily and said, "Hey sweetheart. Are you sitting with us?"

Sofia didn't want to have an ugly confrontation with them but from experience she knew that drunk guys like them could be trouble.

"No. I just need to get past."

As soon as she spoke the other two stopped what they were doing and turned their attention to Sofia. She also saw them exchange a wink with each other.

"Aww, come on," the first guy insisted. "Why do you want to sit somewhere else on your own when you can stay with us?"

He stepped closer to her as he spoke so that their bodies were almost touching. On a crowded plane in a narrow aisle it felt closer than usual. The other two guys also took a step forward, totally blocking Sofia's way.

For a split second she wondered whether she should turn around and go and get one of the cabin crew to help her.

But suddenly she felt a hand on her waist from behind and a familiar voice said, "Have you found our seats yet?"

It was the dirty blonde guy playing the role of male partner.

Without missing a beat, she said, 'No. These guys won't let me through."

The first guy spoke quickly. "Sorry mate. Didn't see you there," He stepped aside and waved his hand graciously for Sofia and her partner to pass.

As she stepped forward the other two also moved out of the way and each gave a slight nod of apology to the dirty blonde guy as he followed her. "Keep walking," he whispered to her, keeping his hand on her waist.

"Thank you so much," she said to him once they were safely past and out of ear shot.

"Don't mention it. I could see you were outnumbered," He dropped his hand from her waist.

"This is me," she said finding her seat on the right. "Looks like I've got a window seat."

"Lucky you. See you later." He carried on to look for his own seat.

Sofia took off the small backpack she was carrying and sat in her seat. She took an eReader from the bag before stowing it under the seat in front of her.

Looking at the two empty seats next to her she wondered who would be sitting with her for the trip and hoped they wouldn't be too chatty.

On her eReader she had some eBooks to read and audio books to listen to as well as some music for meditation and for sleeping. One was to block out the noise and help her think and the other for if she had trouble sleeping in a strange place.

As it turned out, no one was sitting in the seats next to her which suited her just fine.

It felt both exciting and scary to take this trip. Exciting because she'd never done this before and scary for the same reason.

When the doors closed and the plane took off there was no turning back. This was it. Two weeks in Corfu with nothing to do but sit and think.

Sofia stared out the window as the plane soared higher and higher, taking her further and further away from home. She watched until the ground disappeared and all she could see were the clouds.

The cabin crew had performed their safety demonstration before take off and now that they were in the air and the plane was level, they came around selling items from the airline's gift catalogue and then came around again serving a meal.

The flight was over three hours long so Sofia was glad that she was going to get something to eat.

"Vegetarian meal?" The female crew member with the overly-bright red lipstick asked her.

"Yes. Thank you."

The flight attendant put a tray of food on Sofia's drop-down table and moved on.

Sofia inspected what was in the covered containers then settled down to enjoy her potatoes, roast vegetables and beans.

When she'd finished eating and the tray had been taken away, she put her earbuds in and listened to her meditation music as she stared out of the window.

She'd turned off her mobile phone while she was at the airport and had decided not to turn it back on. If she was going to be away for two weeks it may as well be a complete break. Besides, she didn't want to talk to Jason. He was the reason she was here in the first place because it was the only way she could get enough time to think about their relationship and whether or not she wanted to stay with him.

They had been dating for three years now. Jason was thirty three , three years older than Sofia.

They had never lived together, both preferring to keep separate residences, especially Sofia.

She had been married before. She was working as a legal assistant when she met her husband who was a lawyer at the firm they both worked for.

They married while Sofia was only nineteen. But after six years her husband's arrogance became too much to bear and Sofia left him.

They sold their large house and with the money she received from the sale, plus an inheritance from her grandmother who died around the same time, Sofia found herself in the enviable position of being able to buy a house outright with no mortgage.

So she quit her job and began her own company making custom, handmade wedding dresses.

Sofia had always been good at sewing, knitting and crocheting and loved to do it. And she'd already made a couple of wedding dresses for two ex-colleagues and had sat for hours hand-sewing on every single bead and sequin.

After that she received other orders so her business had taken off quite rapidly. Brides were willing to wait months and pay thousands for the right dress.

But Jason had never been supportive of her work and never wanted to talk about it. He was a builder and always liked to explain in detail about how hard he worked, while at the same time implying that what Sofia did every day wasn't work.

Sofia's older sister was also of the same opinion and acted as though Sofia never worked. And whenever her sister mentioned that she had a job Sofia would say "I have a job too you know." But her sister would say it wasn't "proper" work.

And it was the same with her parents. They'd always discuss her sister's job at the bank but never asked Sofia about her work.

Her friends, on the other hand, were extremely supportive and always called round for coffee while she worked. They'd sit and marvel at her ability to sew every bead in exactly the right place and an equal distance from the others.

But Jason, like her family, didn't respect her work. And recently it seemed that Jason didn't respect her at all.

It had all come to a head a month ago and their relationship had been stormy ever since with Jason trying to make up for what he'd said and Sofia unable to forgive him.

It happened at a local pub. They'd gone out for a drink and had run into some of Jason's work mates.

Sofia was hoping for a quiet night out for two, but Jason seemed elated to see his mates and so they all sat together.

Naturally the conversation turned to work so Sofia couldn't join in. The men talked work jargon for over thirty minutes. She knew it was that long because she had nothing to do except stare at the clock on the wall. Several times she tried to interject and change the conversation but they all acted as though she wasn't there. Jason even sat with his back half turned towards her.

After precisely thirty four minutes and five seconds, she'd had enough of being ignored. She wasn't having a good time and would be happier at home doing her sewing and watching a movie.

So she stood up and left.

She hadn't gotten far outside the door when Jason grabbed her arm from behind.

"What the hell is wrong with you?" he growled.

"Wrong with me?" she asked, whirling around and pulling her arm from his grasp. "You turned your back and completely ignored me for over half an hour."

"I was taking to my mates. It's not my fault you were sulking."

She couldn't believe what she was hearing.

"Sulking? Is that what you call it?" She was seething but tried to keep her voice quiet and calm. "You guys have talked about nothing but work. How the hell can I join in the conversation if I don't have a clue what you're all talking about?"

"How could you understand anything about work conversations? When was the last time we ran into some of your work mates? Oh that's right," he jeered, snapping his fingers, "you don't have any."

"Let's not start that old argument again. I do work for a living but unlike you I don't have to go out to do it."

He gave a short derisive laugh.

Sofia cut him off before he could say anything. "You know what? I'm so sick and tired of your jealousy. You can't stand how amazing my job is. Why else would you hate it so much? You're simply jealous."

"And you're embarrassing," he spat back. "I'm trying to have a good time with my mates and you're showing me up with your childish display of storming out when you can't get my attention. It's not me that's jealous, it's you. You just can't stand it if you don't have all my attention to yourself."

At that moment something shifted in Sofia's emotions and the only feeling she had for Jason was one of contempt.

He must have seen it too because as he stared at her, his expression changed from one of mocking arrogance to surprise.

"Sofia I'm sorry." He grabbed both her arms, but she shook him off as he continued. "I shouldn't have said any of that. I'm sorry. You were right, I was ignoring you and not including you in the conversation."

"I know damn well I was right. And I didn't storm out, I just left. And now I simply want to go home."

"Sofia I'm sorry."

"You always are."

"Come back inside and I promise, PROMISE that I won't ignore you."

But Sofia didn't want to be with him anymore, and at that moment she wasn't sure if that feeling was just for that night or permanently.

"Jason, I'm tired. I'm tired of all our petty arguments and your total lack of respect for me and everything I do.

"I get it, you know, I really do. You work hard for living and by comparison my life must be enviable because it looks like I never work. But I do and I'm fortunate that my hobby is also how I earn money. And if you have a problem with that then it's your problem and I don't want it to be my problem anymore. I've had enough of your disrespect and put-downs and tonight is just more of it." She felt weary and just wanted to go.

Jason must have subconsciously known it too. "Look Sofia, we'll talk tomorrow."

"No we won't. I don't want to stomp over the same ground with you. I've had enough. You win. You don't respect what I do and you never will."

"No you're wrong," he pleaded. "I do respect what you do. But I have to get back to my mates now. I'll come by tomorrow and we'll talk."

"Sure." Sofia turned and walked away.

She couldn't believe it. There she was wondering if she should end their three year relationship there and then and he thought that getting back to his mates was more important.

The next day he did come round and try and convince her that he had the utmost respect for her custom-made bridal gown business, but they both knew it was a lie.

That was when Sofia decided to book a holiday and get far away and give herself time to think. She was sure that Jason meant what he said and that he'd never criticise what she did again, but she also knew that he didn't respect her work. He never would. The question was whether she could live with that unspoken disrespect.

And as the plane began its decent to Corfu International Airport, the scenery coming into view became a stark reminder of what a foreign place she was entering, and how alone she was, and she felt butterflies in her stomach.

After the plane landed, she stood nervously at the luggage carousel waiting for her suitcase to make itself known to her from all the others.

She looked up and saw that the dirty blonde guy was stood opposite her. He had obviously already seen her because he was looking directly at her and smiling. She suddenly wondered if that smile was permanent because so far she hadn't seen him with any other expression.

She returned his smile and he immediately looked happier, if that was possible.

Her suitcase came into view and she grabbed it as it passed by on the conveyor belt. She put it on the floor beside her, pulled out the handle and wheeled it away, waving goodbye to the dirty blonde guy as she headed off to find the bus that would be taking her to her destination.

When her suitcase was safely stowed in the luggage compartment under the bus, she got on board and chose a seat four rows back from the front.

There were only two other people on board so she gazed out the window watching others approach.

The driver, was standing below her window asking passengers where they were staying before stowing their luggage in the right place.

As the bus began to fill she saw the dirty blonde guy approaching. He was smiling at the driver as he walked up.

"Which hotel?" asked the driver with a deep, Greek accent.

"Ionia Bianco," said the dirty blonde guy.

"Interesting," she thought to herself. "We're staying at the same place. Looks like I haven't seen the last of him yet."

He scanned the bus for a spare seat as he boarded and his smile broadened when he saw Sofia looking at him. She couldn't help but smile back.

He sat in the seat directly across the aisle from her.

Soon everyone was aboard, the luggage compartment was slammed shut, the driver and the tour representative got on board and the final leg of the journey began.

Whenever the bus pulled up at a hotel or resort the dirty blonde guy watched her anxiously to see if she was going to get off. When there was only a few passengers left and the driver announced the next stop was the last at Iona Bianco, he looked relieved and beaming at her he said, "Looks like we're going to be neighbours."

But at that point neither of them realised how close their rooms would be with only one other in between.

*

"Yasoo." The sudden greeting jolted her out of her reverie.

"Yasoo," she replied, standing up. Finally, someone to fix her electric problem.

The man took one step inside her room, turned to a small metal box high up on the wall just inside the door, opened it and clicked the trip switch back up.

He then closed the box, muttered a quick "Goodnight," and left.

Sofia felt both relieved to have the electricity back on and annoyed that it was so simple to fix yet she'd waited an hour for it to happen. If she'd have known about the meter box she'd have flipped the switch herself.

She walked into her room. The door led directly into a small kitchen. A door to the left led into a small bathroom. Beyond the kitchen was the bedroom/living room which contained a double bed with a small sofa backing onto the end of it, a built-in wardrobe backing onto the bathroom wall, a desk with drawers down both sides and a small TV was on the wall opposite the bed and sofa.

At the opposite end of the room was a sliding glass door. Sofia walked over to it, slid it open and stepped out onto the patio which contained only a small plastic table and two plastic chairs.

She went back inside, closed the door and drew the heavy curtains.

After unpacking she had a shower, put on her nightdress, which looked like an extra-long T-shirt, and made herself something to eat.

She'd brought a few things with her including instant noodles and crackers and right now she was so hungry that such simple, unhealthy food seemed appetising.

Once she boiled the noodles, she sat on the sofa, ate them with the crackers and skipped through the TV channels to see what was on. Some channels were Greek but most were English.

But once she finished eating all she wanted to do was sleep, so she took her bowl and fork to the kitchen, drank a glass of water and went to bed.

She took out her eReader and read for a short while before falling asleep.

Sadly though, she didn't sleep for long because she soon heard loud voices and the unmistakable sound of suitcase wheels rumbling across tiled floors. And the sounds were all coming from the room next to hers.

"Finally, we're here!" yelled a male voice.

"I'm pooped." said a female. "Let's go get a drink."

"Perhaps we should unpack first."

"No way! I'm on holiday. I want to have fun."

"It won't seem like fun when you have to come back and unpack after a few drinks."

"Fine. I'll unpack tomorrow. Now please can we go enjoy ourselves?"

There was a brief silence before the man responded. "Sure. I guess. But we'll be sorry later." And with that the door closed and footsteps could be heard passing Sofia's door and continuing along the path.

Sofia closed her eyes but it seemed to take a while before she could fall asleep again. Her mind felt unsettled.

"What have I done? Is this the biggest mistake of my life?" Well if coming here was a mistake she had two whole weeks to regret it.

But she decided that it probably wouldn't be too bad no matter what.

All she'd come here to do was relax, sew, knit, read and think. She had her own room to hide away in and if the neighbours were too noisy, she had her music to plug into her ears. And during the day she could go to the beach or sit by the pool and read.

There was also supposed to be a few shops and local restaurants nearby.

Yes. She'd be fine, she assured herself. It would be a quiet, relaxing holiday.

Little did she know that this two week vacation was going to change her life.

Chapter 2 - Saturday Morning

The next morning Sofia woke to see the sun shining around the edges of the heavy patio curtains.

She turned onto her back, put her arms above her head and stretched before reaching out to the night stand for her watch. Five minutes past eight.

How had she slept so long? And she must have slept deeply because she hadn't heard her neighbours return last night.

She looked around the room and breathed in the musty smell. It felt exciting to wake up somewhere new.

She'd never been on holiday alone before, apart from a few weekend getaways back in England, and she thought she'd feel anxious on her first day here but it actually felt exciting.

She got out of bed, walked barefoot across the room, opened the curtains, slid open the patio door and stepped outside.

Her patio looked out onto a garden.

All the other rows of rooms were staggered so that no patio faced directly onto another and the garden provided enough space so no others were too close to hers.

There was a row of four rooms to her left, at the far side of the main path.

Another group of rooms was opposite hers but they were facing diagonally to the right so all she could see was one end wall. Sofia thought it was great that when she sat on her patio no one would be directly facing her and there was a full-sized wall between her and her neighbours' patio.

Leaving the door and curtains open, she went back inside, switched on the TV, selected a news channel and headed for the bathroom.

The shower felt good. Because the day was so warm already, she chose to wear a pair of black shorts and a white, embroidered, loose shirt.

She had breakfast indoors, with the curtains and door still open. It was a simple breakfast of toast and coffee using the bread rolls and coffee that she'd brought with her and a small pat of margarine that she'd kept from her meal on the plane.

She turned off the TV, poured herself a second cup of coffee from the two cup coffee press that she'd found in one of the kitchen cupboards, and went to sit outside.

The sky was a perfect blue without a cloud in sight.

It was now nine o'clock and there was a welcome meeting in an hour for new guests. She knew that from a leaflet that she'd received in an information pack with her ticket. There'd also been other helpful things in it like a description of the area and all the amenities at the resort. It said the beach was accessible through the pool area which was fenced off to keep young children out.

Her plan for the morning was to attend the meeting (in an upstairs meeting room above the bar, apparently) and then laze by the pool for a while.

"Oh hi. You must be our neighbour." The sudden voice made her jump. She turned to see a woman of around forty five to fifty years old standing on the lawn in front of the dividing wall.

The woman gestured to the room next door. "We just arrived last night."

"Yes. So I heard."

"Oh sorry. Were we too loud? I knew it was a bad idea to start banging around unpacking late at night after we'd had a few drinks."

Sofia hadn't heard any unpacking and thought that she must have slept more deeply than she realised. She also nearly answered back "I thought you said you'd unpack in the morning?" but decided against it because it might sound as though she was nosey and had been listening through the wall on purpose. Instead she just smiled.

The woman stepped forward and took a step up onto Sofia's patio. "Hi. I'm Lenore. I'm here with my husband Mick."

"Hi Lenore. I'm Sofia."

"No husband?" Lenore enquired, looking past Sofia and into her room.

"No, it's just me on my own on a getting-away-from-it-all break."

"Good for you. It looks like a nice place to do it."

Sofia looked out over the garden. "I don't know yet. I only arrived last night too."

"Oh really? We're here for two weeks."

"Me too."

"How wonderful. We can be holiday neighbours."

Lenore then talked uninterrupted for the next few minutes telling Sofia her life story.

It seemed that Lenore and Mick had retired early and wanted to travel for a few years. They'd already been to Greece for two weeks and now they'd arrived in Corfu and from what Sofia could gather they were both in their fifties.

"I should introduce you to Mick." Lenore stepped back down onto the grass while shouting, "Come and meet our new neighbour!"

A familiar voice replied, "Don't mind if I do."

Lenore laughed and said to the person that Sofia couldn't yet see, "Oh, are you our neighbour on the other side?"

"What did you say," said another deeper male voice.

"Lenore smiled and said, "I was just telling you to come and meet our new neighbour at this side but I didn't see this young man here and it turns out he's our neighbour at the other side. So why don't we all come over here and meet each other?" She gestured towards Sofia's patio.

Lenore turned and came back up to Sofia and from around the corner came the dirty blonde guy and another older man who had to be Mick.

The dirty blonde guy smiled widely at Sofia. "Hi neighbour."

Sofia couldn't help but smile broadly in return. But before she could respond Lenore cut her off.

"So let's do the introductions. I'm Lenore and this is my husband, Mick," she said grabbing onto the older man's arm. "We just arrived last night and we're here for a fortnight."

Mick nodded once in greeting. He was a tall thick set man with dark hair and a neatly trimmed moustache. Sofia had the feeling that he was a man of few words which complimented his extremely chatty wife.

"Your turn," Lenore said to the dirty blonde guy.

"My name's Ted. I arrived yesterday too and I'm here for a couple of weeks as well."

"Are you here with your wife?"

Ted laughed. "Ha, no. I divorced her last week."

"Oh I'm sorry."

"Don't be. It was a much better idea than marrying her."

"Oh...OK." Lenore turned to Sofia. "And this, I just found out, is Sofia and she's here for two weeks too." Sofia raised one hand and gave a brief wave to the men. Ted smiled at her and Mick nodded.

"I know," said Lenore, clapping her hands together, "Why don't we all sit down and have coffee together. We can bring a couple of extra chairs over here."

Sofia didn't like that idea at all. She was grateful to meet more people so that she didn't feel so alone here, but being so social so soon isn't what she wanted at all. She had planned a quiet day on her own getting to know her way around.

Thankfully she had a legitimate excuse to say no. "I'd love to but I haven't got time right now. I want to go to the welcome meeting and it starts soon."

Lenore didn't seem at all upset by the rejection. "Not to worry. We can do it later. Mick and I aren't bothered about the meeting but we'll let you go if you want to."

"You'll LET me go?" thought Sofia. She had thought that Lenore had a dominating type of personality when she first spoke to her and now she knew she was right.

Sofia stood up and picked up her coffee cup. "OK. No doubt we'll all catch up with each other later. After all, we're here for a fortnight."

Lenore laughed and clapped her hands together again. "It's going to be such fun." She turned to Mick. "Come on. Let's go back to our room and you can make us a cup of coffee."

Mick nodded at Sofia then turned and left with his wife.

Ted watched them go and turned back to Sofia. "I'd better go too."

"Me too. I have to get ready. Nice meeting you." She turned to go back inside her room.

Ted stepped down off her patio with a cheery, "See you later," and was gone.

After washing and drying the dishes and getting changed, Sofia headed off to the welcome meeting.

Before she left she changed into her bikini and wore it under a light, long-sleeved white, cotton shirt. The shirt was designed to be worn as a beach cover-up or as a top. Sofia also put on a pair of floral shorts and carried her beach bag which contained a few necessities and her towel.

She headed towards the reception building because she knew that was where the bar was, and the meeting room above. A shop, a cafe and a restaurant were also situated there.

She went into the shop first and bought a bottle of water before heading up to the meeting.

There was a female holiday company representative greeting everyone as they entered and handing out paper packages

A few dozen chairs had been set out in four rows. Sofia chose a middle seat in the second last row.

Once she was seated she started looking through all the papers in the package she'd been given and saw that most were leaflets about local attractions plus there was a form listing them all, the cost of going, and a space to book to go. There was also a list of dos and don'ts to help visitors understand and fit in with the local culture.

She looked through the activities on offer but none really appealed to her. She didn't want to go on an all-day boat trip or a visit to a water park with one of the world's biggest slides.

But there was a day trip to the island's capital, Corfu Town. It wasn't a guided tour or anything, just a bus trip there in the morning and being brought back again in the afternoon. The buses were every Sunday, so she could go tomorrow or next Sunday.

She looked up and saw that all the chairs were now nearly all taken, including one next to her. She must have been so engrossed in reading that she hadn't noticed them sit down. It was a middle aged man and he was talking to the woman beside him who must be his wife.

Then she saw a familiar smiling face enter the room.

Ted took a package from the woman at the door and then scanned the room. When he saw Sofia his smile widened. She couldn't help but smile back. He certainly seemed like an easy-going, happy guy.

Ted made his way to the back row and sat behind Sofia.

"Welcome everyone. My name is Wendy and I'll be your company representative throughout your stay here at Ionia Bianco." All eyes turned to the woman at the front of the room.

Sofia recognised her as the same person who had greeted everyone at the airport and directed them to the right bus and had then ridden along with them.

The woman talked on for a while about all the amenities at the hotel, the shops, bars and restaurants in the local area and the nightlife available in the nearby town of Kavos where there were several night clubs.

Then she talked about the activities and attractions that were available through the company.

Sofia listened as she described them all but still none appealed to her except the bus trip to Corfu Town.

Before handing in her form at the end of the meeting she filled out her name, room number and phone number for the trip to Corfu Town the next day. She figured that if she went on the first Sunday and enjoyed it, she could always book to go again the following Sunday.

She queued up, handed in her form, paid the money for it, and left.

Her plan was to spend a couple of hours at the pool which was close to the main building and she could already hear the "pool noises" of shouting and splashing.

The pool area was completely fenced in with pool safety fencing and child safety gates.

She entered and looked around. There was one huge pool that had a humped bridge over each end plus a small children's pool beside it. At the far end of the big pool was an open-air bar with stools all around it plus plenty of tables and chairs, all under one big roof.

Sofia made her way around to the far side of the big pool looking for a quieter place to sit away from the children's pool where all the parents and young kids had congregated in one, huge, noisy group.

The fence at the far side of the pool was a six foot wire fence with barbed wire at the top and it had a gate that opened straight onto the beach. According to the brochures, it was possible to walk along the beach to Kavos as well as walking on the main road. She would try both at some point. Right now though, all she wanted was somewhere to sit.

There were many white plastic sun loungers around the pool. Sofia chose one that wasn't too close to other people. She laid her towel out on it, stripped down to her bikini, stored her belongings in the shade under the lounger, and stretched out on it in the sun.

As she closed her eyes she had an immediate feeling of bliss. It felt so good to feel the warmth of the sun on her body, and the constant sounds around her of people enjoying themselves was soothing. She hadn't felt this relaxed since she got out of bed yesterday morning. That was probably why it felt so good now to be finally doing what she came here to do.

Her planned holiday was one of relaxation but so far it had seemed nothing like that. But at least she was here now and the resort seemed OK so far. Her room was clean and comfortable and her neighbours were friendly, especially Ted, the perpetual smiling guy.

Then she remembered that Ted had been sitting behind her at the meeting but she hadn't spoken to him. In fact, she'd been so busy thinking about booking the trip to Corfu Town that she'd forgotten he was there.

Oh dear. Had he thought that she'd ignored him on purpose?

Well, she reasoned to herself, it didn't matter if he did or didn't. He had said that he was newly divorced and so was probably looking for a rebound relationship so she'd do well to not encourage his attention too much.

And besides she was already in a relationship and had been for 3 years. Although it wasn't a happy relationship and that was why she'd come away to put some distance between them and give them both time to think about if it was worth saving or call it a day and go their own separate ways.

Sofia admitted to herself that not having Jason in her life anymore appealed to her more than continuing to see him. What she'd really done by coming here was to escape from him and give herself time to figure out how she was going to tell him goodbye and get him to accept it.

Right now she felt that she would be happy to stay in Corfu forever and never have to go back.

Wow! Was that how much she disliked being with Jason that she'd give up her whole life as she knew it just to never have to see him again? Boy, her thoughts were going deep all of a sudden, or maybe it was being so relaxed that had allowed these repressed thoughts to surface.

She knew she had to face it. Their relationship was over and she would have to end it as soon as she returned home. She just had to think of how to say it. "Well Jason, I was on holiday alone and thinking that I was glad you weren't with me and that made me realise that I don't want you with me at all." The thought almost made her smile.

"Mind if I sit here?"

The sudden voice broke off her thoughts abruptly. She knew that now familiar voice straight away.

Using her hand to shade her eyes before she opened them she said, "Sure. Do what you want."

Ted was already laying his towel on the sun lounger beside her. Had he been looking for her or had he simply stumbled across her?

She had a momentary feeling of unease because she didn't want him to think that she was at all interested in him romantically.

On the other hand maybe he wasn't looking for that either and simply wanted to sit with her because she was the only person he knew here.

He stretched out beside her and put his hands behind his head. He was wearing only a pair of dark blue Speedos. His body was slim but muscular and his shaggy hair fell back across his wrists, revealing his face even more. Sofia took a good look at him as he gazed up at the cloudless sky.

She found him very easy on the eyes. His personality seemed easy-going too. He struck her as a man who doesn't let things get him down.

"It's beautiful here, isn't it?" he asked.

"I'm loving it here so far," she said.

Ted turned to look at her "What made you choose this place."

She thought about it for a moment. "Because it looked like it had everything I needed plus it's far away from everything without being too far. Like Kavos for example. It's supposed to be only a twenty minute walk away during the day, and is supposed to be really quiet without all the night club stuff that goes on at night."

"That's exactly what I thought as well," he said, beaming. "Nice and quiet but not too far from other things. Plus I thought that the pool and beach being so close together was a bonus."

"Do you plan to swim a lot?"

"No. Well...maybe a bit. But mostly I just wanted to come here and chill."

"Me too," she agreed. "I just wanted to relax and get away for a while so the beach and pool seemed pretty attractive. I brought my eReader with me and I got it loaded up with new books before I came."

"Wow, you are prepared for a quiet holiday." He reached down and picked up a thick paperback novel. "I brought this one and another almost as big. I'm not as technologically advanced as you with my reading."

"Aren't you into computers much?"

He laughed. "On the contrary. I love computers. It's what I do for a living. I'm just old fashioned with my reading."

"What do you do with computers?"

"I program them."

Sofia was impressed. Computer programming couldn't be an easy job. "Do you work for yourself?"

"No. I work in London for one of the big banks."

"Wow. Do you live there too?"

"At the bank? No." He laughed at his own joke. Sofia laughed too.

Ted continued. "I do live in London though, in Holland Park."

Again Sofia was impressed. "That's quite an expensive place to live. And it's beautiful too."

"Yes, that's true on both points," he agreed. "I live there because it is so beautiful there and I can afford it because I don't spend a lot of money on other things so last year I bought a mews house there."

"But aren't you newly divorced? What about your ex-wife?"

"She lives in an apartment in Earls Court. We split up over two years ago. Before the split, we'd been married for ten years, since I was twenty and we found out she was pregnant. We thought getting married was the right thing to do, but it turns out we were wrong."

"And the child?"

"Miscarriage."

"I'm sorry." Sofia couldn't imagine him ever looking sad. But she now knew how old he was, if he married his pregnant wife at twenty and had been married ten years and separated for two years, that made him thirty two. Two years older than herself.

Ted went on to tell her how difficult his ex-wife had been once they'd separated.

It seemed that she was quite the snob and was infuriated when Ted left her and took his high-paying job with him.

He paid her regular money for a while and left her with all their furniture and household belongings, taking nothing but his personal items.

She'd taken him to court to try and claim ongoing alimony for herself but Ted had hired a top lawyer to argue that his ex-wife could get a job if she wanted to so there was no need for him to financially support her. She was also being difficult over their previous marital home and was refusing to sign any papers so that they could sell it.

Sofia was surprised he was still smiling as he spoke. "Does nothing ever get you down?"

"Sure. But I never stay there. Where's the fun in that?"

She liked his easy-breezy attitude. It was the complete opposite of Jason who always seemed like he was looking for the next argument.

Ted looked over at the pool and then back at Sofia. "Fancy a swim?"

She smiled and nodded. They walked over to the edge of the pool together. Ted held her hand and they jumped in.

The water felt good. They swam for a while, then sunbathed in companionable silence and swam again.

Ted shook his hair to dry it a bit and laid back down on his sun lounger after their second swim.

Sofia sat and towelled her long hair. She took out her watch which was still stowed safely in the shade under her lounger.

"Wow it's two o'clock already. I'm going to go back to my room for a while."

They gathered their belongings and walked back together, chatting amicably as they went. Sofia had wrapped her towel around herself and tucked it in securely under her left arm.

Ted was such an easy person to be with. He smiled constantly, laughed often and looked cute with his damp, blonde ringlets, hanging messily down to just above his shoulders and glinting in the sun as he walked.

They stopped at Sofia's door. "Thanks Ted. I enjoyed it."

"Yeah, I am fun to be with," he said, grinning.

Sofia feigned annoyance at his pretend arrogance. "Goodbye Ted." As she spoke she turned the key in her lock, stepped inside and closed the door, hearing Ted give a small laugh as she did so.

Inside her room it was warm. She thought about walking through to the patio door opposite and opening it, but then she decided not to. She wanted to take a shower so thought it best to keep the door locked.

So she picked up the remote control, put on the air conditioning and went to have a shower.

The warm water felt good as it washed away the smell of the chlorinated pool water from her hair and body. As it cascaded over her she could feel the familiar tingling of warm water on sunburnt skin. Looking down she could see the white skin from where her bikini had covered the small area of her body. "The one thing about meeting someone on holiday," she thought to herself, "is that they quickly get to see what your body looks like."

She then thought about how good Ted looked in his Speedos, and smiled to herself.

Once showered she towelled herself dry, put on fresh underwear, the pair of black cotton shorts and the white embroidered top she'd worn earlier, and blow dried her hair.

She rinsed out her bikini and hung it over one of the chairs on the patio and hung her towel over the other.

Then she slipped into a pair of flat shoes, turned off the air conditioning, grabbed her handbag and headed off to the local shops.

There wasn't much around in the small village but there was a grocery store as well as three restaurants that each had a bar.

She sat and had a cold glass of orange juice at one of them. It felt so pleasant to sit there in the warm afternoon shade, freshly showered after a swim and a sunbathe, with nothing much to do for the rest of the day.

She took in everything around her, enjoying how different it was from her home in Bath.

The TV was on in the bar and she could see it from her outside table but she couldn't hear it. The program was a British comedy show which she'd seen before, so she watched it in silence, already knowing what would happen next.

When she'd finished her juice she headed to the grocery store picked up a shopping basket, and browsed every aisle, gathering a few items in her basket as she went.

Some of the groceries she recognised. Others she couldn't quite figure out what they were and the Greek writing on the labels didn't help.

She chose a big packet of potato chips and a bottle of wine, added them to her basket and made her way to the checkout.

Back in her room she stored her groceries in the one small kitchen cupboard and in the small fridge. She also put her wine in there to chill.

Then she threw herself on the bed, switched on the air conditioner and the TV and flicked through the channels until she found a movie to watch.

It felt so decadent to be laid there doing absolutely nothing, all alone and no responsibilities for the rest of the day. No Jason insisting that they spend the evening together even if she didn't want to. Now she had every evening to herself for two whole weeks.

"Yikes!" She thought to herself. "I feel so happy to be away from him. That's a sign that I really shouldn't be with him."

She closed her eyes.

When she opened them the room was dark. The only light was from the TV. How long had she been asleep?

She sat up, rubbed her eyes, reached out, switched on the bedside lamp and looked at her watch. It was five minutes past eight. Wow. She'd been asleep for a while.

She put on the light, went outside to retrieve her bikini and towel, locked the door and closed the curtains behind her and then headed for the shower.

Back in the bedroom she put on her nightie and went to the kitchen to make some dinner.

She dined simply on baked beans on toast while sitting cross legged on her bed watching TV.

Once she'd washed and dried the dishes she came back into the main room with the bag of potato chips and a big glass of wine.

She found a comedy series that she liked on TV, propped herself up with the four pillows on her bed, and felt luxurious yet slothful as she slumped back and drank wine and ate chips.

Because she'd already slept for a few hours she thought she'd be unable to fall asleep early. But within an hour she felt herself getting sleepy. So when she finished her wine she turned off the air conditioner, the lights and the TV, jumped under the covers and was soon asleep.

As she drifted off she thought about Ted and how much she'd enjoyed being at the pool with him. But she didn't want to encourage him to be with her too much because she was still in a relationship with someone else and wanted (and needed) to have the quiet holiday that she'd planned.

Tomorrow was the trip to Corfu Town that she'd booked at the welcome meeting. The bus was leaving at ten o'clock so she'd be able to go straight out after breakfast and avoid running into Ted all day.

Yep, a quiet day in Corfu town would be just what she needed.

Chapter 3 - Sunday

Sofia awoke to another bright, sunny day.

She woke up early at 6 a.m. and laid in bed watching the Greek news until 8 a.m. and then got up and went to the bathroom to use the toilet and brush her teeth.

She didn't open the curtains until she'd gotten dressed, put away her clothes from yesterday and made her breakfast.

She'd dressed in a long, black cotton skirt with an elastic waist and patterned with small lilac flowers. She paired it with a simple white, sleeveless top with a V neck.

When her breakfast was ready she opened the curtains, slid open the patio door, and carried her porridge and orange juice out to the table.

It felt so wonderful and free to be sitting in such a beautiful garden setting on a warm, sunny day with nothing much going on in life.

When she'd finished her breakfast she took her dishes into the kitchen and came back with a cup of coffee.

As she sat and enjoyed her longed-for alone time, she realised how calm she now felt about coming here alone compared to how nervous she felt two days ago, before she came.

Two days ago? Is that all it had been?

She'd set off on Friday morning and today was only Sunday, yet she was already so settled here that it felt as though she belonged here now.

She left her room at five minutes to ten and went to the reception where the bus was supposed to pick everyone up. It was waiting when she got there and many people were already seated on board.

Sofia climbed aboard and looked for a seat. Most were taken.

About halfway up she saw a woman with a small child sitting on her lap. Sofia headed for the empty seat beside her.

As she approached she caught a glimpse of the now familiar blonde ringlets, two rows farther back on the other side.

She looked across to see him smiling at her. It felt comforting to see a familiar face in a sea of strangers so she couldn't help but give a genuine smile in return before taking her seat.

The bus journey didn't seem to take long. Sofia enjoyed looking at the unfamiliar scenery outside the window while talking to her temporary companion in the seat beside her.

It seemed the woman was a single parent who had come on a two week holiday with a friend who was also a single parent. But immediately on arriving it turned out that she and her friend couldn't agree on anything including which activities and days out to take part in or whether their two children should spend every day at the on-site childcare centre or stay with them. The woman wanted to spend more time with her child while her friend wanted to ditch the kids as much as possible.

Sofia had no opinion to offer but listening to the woman's woes and watching her child throw up in a travel sick bag the whole way made her thankful that she wasn't travelling with a small child herself. It didn't look or sound like fun.

Before she knew it the bus turned in the opposite direction and swung round and parked in it's designated spot at a large bus station.

The driver announced that he would be leaving the exact same spot at 5 pm so everyone had to make sure they were back by then.

As he spoke, Sofia's companion squeezed past her, carrying her still-vomiting child and quickly made her way off the bus. Sofia was grateful to get rid of the sound and smell the child was producing.

She waited her turn to leave the bus. Once outside she retrieved the leaflet from her handbag that contained a map of Corfu Town.

"So, where shall we go first?" Ted was standing beside her and spoke with the natural assumption that they were together for the day.

"We?" she asked, trying not to show her surprise.

He shrugged good-naturedly. "Why not? Neither of us know anyone else here and there's always safety in numbers."

She had to admit that it made sense. They were in a foreign country so it would be safer to stick together than to wander around alone.

But having someone with her meant that she wouldn't be free to explore only places of her own choosing or to linger as long she wanted.

But she could always come back next Sunday on her own if she saw something interesting.

"OK then." She scanned their immediate surroundings. They were standing next to a park and across the road was a cafe. She pointed to the cafe and then to the park. "How about we get a coffee there and drink it there."

"Sounds good to me." He took hold of her hand and together they crossed the busy road.

There were many cars and buses and also many mopeds. It seemed that the bike riding was popular in Corfu. Horns blared and drivers yelled at each other yet it seemed to be an accepted way to drive with no road rage in sight.

Sofia thought that Ted had taken her hand to guide her across the busy road. But once at the other side he still held her hand as they walked to the cafe, as though it was the most natural thing in the world.

"How do you like your coffee?" he asked her.

"Black. No sugar."

"Me too," he said smiling at her and raising his eyebrows in surprise. Sofia was surprised too because she didn't know anyone else who drank coffee in such a basic state.

"Two medium black coffees to go," he told the woman behind the counter. "No sugar."

"Black?" she asked.

"Yes," he confirmed.

Ted let go of Sofia's hand and took out his wallet.

"I'll pay for mine," she told him.

"No need. You can pay for the next one." Somehow, in a way she couldn't explain, his easy assumption that they would be together long enough for a 'next one' made her happy.

They each carried their cup of coffee to the park across the road. Ted held her hand again as soon as they walked away from the counter. Sofia decided it would be nice to accept Ted's fast, close friendship and just go with it.

They found a shady tree to sit under and sat cross legged side by side, watching everything around them.

They discussed what they should do for the rest of the day and looked at Sofia's map.

After a while of not being able to make up their minds, Ted said, "How about this. We'll just walk wherever we want and see where the day takes us" It was a simple and do-able plan.

"Done," Sofia agreed and put her map back in her bag.

They finished their coffee and spent the next couple of hours wandering the city, going in and out of shops, and holding hands the whole time.

Eventually Ted said, "I'm hungry."

Sofia realised that she was too but hadn't noticed because she was so relaxed and enjoying the day. "Me too.

But I must warn you that I only eat plant-based food. No dead animals or animals products." This was usually the point where people didn't want to eat with her.

"For health or compassionate reasons?"

"Both. But mostly for compassion."

Ted didn't seem to mind at all. "OK we'll stop at the next restaurant we see and tell them that they have to make something you can eat and I'll have the same."

Sofia was touched by his offer to also eat a compassionate meal. "You don't have to have the same."

"I don't mind trying something different. It can be a holiday adventure." He out-stretched his arms to emphasise the last word, but because he was holding Sofia's hand, he slammed her own arm into her chest.

As soon as he realised what he'd done, he let go of her hand and put his arm across her shoulders. Giving her an affectionate squeeze he said, "Sorry," but at the same time he couldn't stop laughing.

Sofia was laughing too. He hadn't hurt her but she had been taken by surprise.

Ted didn't remove his arm as they carried on walking.

They were on a steep hill. At the top they came across a small restaurant with several outside tables and chairs. The tables were covered in red and white checked cloths.

A short, round Greek man greeted them from the doorway."Yasoo," he called to them and gestured at the tables with both hands.

Sofia and Ted looked at each other questioningly. "Why not?" he said.

They sat at one of the tables. The man rushed forward and helped Sofia with her chair. Then he disappeared inside for a minute and returned with a bottle of cold water and two glasses.

He poured a glass for each of them, placed the bottle in the middle of the table and produced two menus from under his arm.

Sofia and Ted looked through the meals on offer. Nearly all of them were meat or fish dishes. Sofia made a suggestion. "There's salad with tomato chutney and crusty rolls. Why don't we order those and a plate of hot chips to share?"

"Sounds good to me. But which salad? There are several listed."

"How about tomato salad."

Ted gestured to the man who had retreated back to stand in the doorway. He returned to their table with pad and pencil in hand. Ted ordered their food and asked Sofia what she'd like to drink.

"I wouldn't mind a cold beer," she told him honestly.

"Excellent," he said clapping his hands to gather. "I was thinking the same."

"Two beer?" the man asked while already writing it on his pad. Ted nodded.

The man took the menus and went back inside.

Soon he brought out their beers in tall, straight glasses. Ted and Sofia chinked their glasses together and said "Cheers," before taking a drink.

Sofia wasn't sure if it was really nice beer or if just being here and feeling so relaxed and happy made it taste nicer than it actually was.

Ted was looking around. They had a nice view from where they were at the top of the steep street. "It is so great being here. I'm loving it."

Sofia looked at the view too. She could see many streets in Corfu Town. "Me too. At first I wondered if a two week holiday alone was going to be too long, but I'm really enjoying it so far."

"I told you yesterday why I'm here alone, to get away from my awful ex-wife and to celebrate my newly divorced status, so what about you?"

"What do you want to know?"

"Well, let's start with where you're from."

"I live in Bath," Sofia told him.

"That must be an expensive place to live."

"Not for me. I split up with my husband several years ago and we had a big house. When we sold it we made a good profit on it, plus my grandmother had died at the same time and she left me quite a bit of money, so I managed to buy a small house for cash."

Ted whistled. "Quite the heiress."

"Oh, not at all," said Sofia, half laughing. "I only bought what I could afford and what I needed. So it's a small two-bedroomed house but it does have a good sized garden."

"You like gardening?"

"Not really. I just like how it keeps me a good distance from my neighbours. I like my privacy."

The man came back and placed two large bowls and one small one in the middle of the table. One large bowl contained the crusty rolls while the other contained many large slices of tomato sprinkled with a few green olives. The small bowl was filled with tomato chutney.

The man disappeared back inside.

Sofia and Ted both leaned forward and peered into the bowl of tomatoes and olives. Then they looked up at each other and burst out laughing. "Doesn't salad mean a combination of different foods tossed together?" asked Ted.

"Well there are olives in there too," offered Sofia. They both laughed again.

The man came back with a bowl of hot chips and two dinner plates.

"Can we have a lettuce salad too please?" Ted asked him.

"Of course," said the man in this thick, Greek accent, then nodded and walked away.

He returned in less than two minutes with a bowl of lettuce leaves with a scattering of olives. "Thank you," Ted said to the man as he turned and left. Then to Sofia he said, "So let's tuck in."

As they began to fill their plates he said, "Continue with your story. Do you have children?"

"No. My husband was a lawyer and very career minded so he wanted to wait a few years until we were financially secure before starting a family. But by that time I didn't want to be with him anymore, let alone have a child with him."

She went on to tell him of how she and her husband met, her handmade bridal gown business and her decaying relationship with Jason and how she'd come here to put some distance between them so that she could have time to think.

Ted listened attentively, interjecting now and again to ask a question or recount similar situations of his own.

Before she knew it, the meal was finished, they'd drank a whole bottle of water and had a second beer each. She felt as though she could sit there forever.

They asked for the bill, both paid equally in cash, used the amenities inside and left.

They made their way hand in hand back down the steep street and meandered slowly back through the city to the bus station. They chatted amicably the whole time. Sofia felt so comfortable being with him that there were moments when she felt like they were a couple.

They were too early for the bus, so they went and sat in the park under the same tree as before.

Sofia's earlier bus companion came up to them with her child who had now stopped vomiting. She sat down and regaled them with her string of complaints and what an awful day she'd had. It seemed that it had taken a while for her son to stop throwing up and even then he still felt ill for almost an hour, so he cried and didn't want to walk anywhere.

Then she'd had to force him to drink a bottle of water because she was worried about him being dehydrated. She moaned on and on about what a rotten day it had been.

Sofia wished she'd be quiet. The woman had complained non-stop on the bus and here she was doing nothing but complain again. No wonder she was single and even her best friend couldn't get along with her.

Ted must have been thinking the same because he suddenly cut her off mid-sentence and said, "Right. It's time to go and wait for the bus." He stood up as he said it. Sofia stood up too. He took her hand, and to the woman he said, "See you later," and walked away, pulling Sofia along with him.

Sofia began to laugh once she thought the woman couldn't hear them. "That was abrupt."

Ted scowled and smiled at the same time. "Is she the kind of person you want to be with?"

"Not at all."

"Me neither. I was sitting there listening to her moan on and on and I suddenly thought, why am I listening to all this negative talk? People like that only exist to bring you down to their level of misery."

"But her son was ill."

"No he wasn't. He was travel sick. I saw him throwing up all the way here on the bus and I wondered why a woman with a child who gets travel sick would bring him on a bus trip without giving him some medication for it first. And do you know why she didn't? So she can complain about it."

Sofia laughed at his logic and had to agree. "Yeah, but it's a shame the kid has to suffer."

"Still no reason for us to have to sit and listen to all that negativity."

Again she couldn't argue with his logic.

They went to the place where the bus had dropped them off and waited for it to return.

On the journey back they sat together and watched the scenery go by. Back at Ionia Bianco they walked back to their rooms together. When they reached Sofia's door Ted said, "I've got a cold bottle of wine in my fridge. Want to come over later and sit outside and help me drink it?"

Sofia was glad he asked. She'd had such a wonderful day that she didn't want it to end. "I'd love to. What time?"

"Whatever time you'd like. Come over when you're ready. Just give me time for a shower and a bite to eat."

"OK. I'll see you soon."

He leaned forward and kissed her on the lips. It was only a quick goodbye kiss yet it sent a shiver of excitement through her whole body. She felt her face flush so she turned quickly and put her key in the lock so that Ted wouldn't see.

"See you soon," he said and carried on to his own door.

Inside, her room was really hot from being closed all day, but she didn't care. She was so happy. She almost waltzed around as she showered and got ready. She thought about having something to eat but couldn't think what to make, so decided to skip dinner.

Instead she sat outside and had a cup of coffee and tried to quiet her excited mind.

It was ridiculous. She'd only met Ted two days ago and now she felt as though she was completely smitten with him. It was childish and she thought she was more mature than that. And now he had invited her for a drink with him. Was he expecting more than that?

Sofia told herself not to be so stupid. It was just a drink or two. Maybe he'd just been enjoying their day together too and just like her he didn't want it to end yet.

She would go to his place and just relax and enjoy the evening. Yeah. Just relax and enjoy it.

She sat and took in the view of the garden at night. People were walking through in all different directions on their way out to enjoy their evening.

It was a warm night so she'd dressed in shorts and T-shirt because they were cool and comfortable.

She went over to Ted's room by walking round to his patio instead of the front door

He was already sitting out reading his novel. He glanced up as she stepped up onto his tiled floor. A smile spread instantly across his face.

"I'm not too early am I?" she asked.

"Nope. I've been waiting hours," he laughed. "Come in and I'll get us a drink."

They went inside together. Ted placed his book on the bedside table before they passed through into his kitchen. She couldn't help but notice that his room was identical to hers in nearly every way.

She placed her door keys on the kitchen counter. It was the only thing she was carrying.

Ted poured two glasses of white wine which they took back out to the patio.

Sofia sat down first and Ted pulled the other chair up beside her. They both sat with their backs to the door.

"I like it here," he told her. "I like the way the garden divides the blocks so that we're not all sat staring at each other."

"I was just thinking the same thing earlier. I also love the way the garden is lit up at night with just enough lights but not too many."

They talked on for a while about everything they liked so far about being there.

"I like it better at night now that you're here," he told her.

"I've been here every night," she said, somewhat confused.

Ted laughed. "You're like a reverse vampire. You only come out in the daytime."

"How do you know where I am at night?"

"The first night I waited for you at the bar after I saw you waiting to get your electricity turned back on. I said I was going there but you never arrived."

"Oh, I was just tired and annoyed that it took an hour for them to turn it on and it turned out it was only the trip switch that needed to be flipped on anyway. So I just went to bed once I'd showered, unpacked and had something to eat."

"Then last night I went to the bar again and waited to see if you'd come. And when you didn't I was going to go to the local bars and see if you were there. But as I was passing your place I went to your door and could hear the TV was on so I figured you were hiding in your room."

Sofia laughed. "I didn't realise I was disappointing you so much. I wasn't hiding. I'd fallen asleep with the TV on. But why were you searching for me? Are you my stalker?"

"Am I creeping you out?" he playfully asked.

"A little."

He threw back his head and laughed. "I never thought I was one of those creepy guys who gets obsessed over a woman and can't leave her alone."

"So why were you stalking me?"

"I just thought it would be nice to sit and chat and get to know you better, that's all. But all's well that ends well and third time lucky because here we are finally."

"So you'll stop stalking me now?"

Ted leaned in close, put his arm around her and said, "I wasn't stalking you and I promise not to start. But there is one thing I'm going to do."

"What's that?"

"Get us both another drink." As he spoke he picked up their empty wine glasses and took them back into the kitchen.

When he came out, he sat back down again and said, "I'm glad you're here tonight." Then he leaned closer and kissed her, only this time it was much more than a quick goodnight kiss.

Sofia returned the kiss while wondering at the same time if she should.

Ted put his hand on Sofia's thigh. His touch felt good, but everything was moving too fast and she needed to slow it down. She pulled away. "We shouldn't."

"Why?" he asked, genuinely perplexed.

But she couldn't immediately think of a reason. "Because we've only known each other a few days?"

"Is that all?" He kissed her again, his hand caressing the inside of her thigh at the same time.

She returned his kiss which was becoming more passionate by the second and for a reason she wasn't sure about, she opened her thighs slightly wider to accommodate his hand, while at the same time wondering how far she was willing to go.

It was too hard to think quickly enough. She broke the kiss and held the hand that was caressing her inner thigh.

They both sat back in their chairs and looked into each other's eyes. Ted didn't say anything and Sofia didn't know him well enough to be able to read his expression. She wondered if he was wounded by her rejection.

A sudden loud voice made them both jump.

"Hey you guys. We've had THE most amazing meal." Lenore stepped onto Ted's patio as she spoke. It was easy to see that she'd had too much to drink. She looked from Sofia's face to Ted's and asked, "Are we interrupting a loving couple?" Mick stepped up beside her and asked, "Sorry, did you two want to be alone?"

Sofia and Ted glanced at each other and then Ted said, "No of course not."

"Are you sure?" Asked Lenore, swaying tipsily. "You both look as though there's more going on. Look how close your chairs are."

Ted gave her one of his easy laughs. "Go get a couple of chairs and join us."

"Why not?" said Lenore, grabbing Mick's hand and dragging him away. They returned in what seemed like a split second with two more plastic chairs. "I'll get us something to drink too." She disappeared again and returned with a bottle of white wine and two glasses.

When their glasses were filled, they all chinked them together over the table and said, "Cheers."

Lenore told them that she and Mick had been out for a meal at one of the local restaurants and had then stayed and had a cocktail or two or three, which explained her somewhat drunken state. Mick looked like he'd had too much to drink too, but he was less chatty so it didn't show as much.

The four of them sat and talked for the next 2 hours and laughed a lot. Lenore was quite funny when she was drunk.

Eventually it was time for bed. Sofia suggested it first saying that she'd had a long day and was tired. Lenore agreed and dragged Mick away.

When they were alone, Ted kissed Sofia goodnight. It was a long and lingering kiss and she couldn't remember the last time she'd felt so aroused. Jason's touch had become somewhat boring to her but she hadn't realised it until Ted's touch and kisses sent a thrill up her spine and down into her loins.

When she walked back into her apartment she closed and locked the door and smiled to herself. She was definitely falling for Ted, even though she knew she shouldn't. Perhaps she needed to cool things down between them a bit.

And thank goodness the neighbours had turned up when they did or Sofia might have ended up doing something she might regret later. Although, being naked in Ted's arms (and his bed) seemed alluring.

But she must stop thinking like that.

Tomorrow she promised herself that she would practice being more aloof.

Chapter 4 - Monday Morning

Sofia opened her curtains to find the sun shining brightly in an almost cloudless sky.

Today she wanted to spend some time at the beach.

Once she showered and dressed she ate a solitary breakfast on her patio while enjoying the sights and sounds of people waking up and going about their leisurely morning business.

Several people stopped briefly to talk to her as they passed by.

A young woman from a nearby apartment opened her patio door, stepped outside and immediately waved. She came across to Sofia's patio. "Hi, I'm Amy," she said cheerfully.

"Hi, I'm Sofia."

"You alone? I saw you a few nights ago dragging your suitcase to the door."

"Yeah, I am."

"I'm here with my boyfriend but he's a late sleeper so you won't see him much in the mornings."

Sofia was surprised to hear that she wasn't here alone because she'd seen her around but she was always by herself. Amy was slim and extremely petite and also very pretty. Sofia wondered why her boyfriend didn't spend much time with her. "I haven't seen him at all," she told Amy.

"Yeah well...he's not a real people person and spends a lot of time alone in front of the TV or on his computer."

"Even on holiday?"

Amy sighed. "Unfortunately, yes."

"That's too bad."

Amy looked uncomfortable and changed the subject. With a bright smile she said, "Well we're neighbours now so no doubt we'll run into each other while we're here."

"I hope so." Sofia felt that she liked Amy, even though she'd only just met her.

"Me too. See ya." And with a quick wave of her hand she was gone.

Sofia made herself a second cup of coffee and drank it inside while she watched the news on TV. Then she washed her dishes and got ready to go to the beach.

She put on a navy blue bikini under a loose dress and packed a towel, a bottle of water and a book in her bag. She usually took her eReader everywhere with her but she didn't want to get sand in it, so she left it behind and packed a paperback novel instead.

It was a gloriously sunny morning but not too hot. Perfect beach weather.

She set off across the complex to the pool area. Once inside the safety fences, she walked over to the far side where there was a gate which opened onto the beach.

There were fewer people on the sand than at the pool.

She walked until she found spot next to a large protruding rock that was far enough away from other people.

She put her bag on the sand, draped her towel over it, took off her dress and sandals and headed straight for the water.

It was cold at first, but she waded in until she was waist deep and then plunged in for a swim. Once she got used to the water, it felt good. She stayed in it longer than she intended, just swimming and lingering and looking out at the mainland of Greece that wasn't far from the island where she was.

There also wasn't much surf, just gentle ripples that lapped at the sand, making it easy to stay in the water.

But soon she noticed the skin on her fingers was pruned so it was time to head back to her towel and read for a while.

She swam back to the shore and made her way out of the water. And as she walked across the sand she saw someone watching her.

As she looked at him she recognised his straggly long blonde hair straight away.

Ted raised his hand and waved while flashing one of his ever-present smiles at her.

Sofia waved back but didn't approach him. Instead she went and dried herself with her towel before spreading it out on the sand and laying on it.

She didn't look back at Ted and wondered if he'd expected her to go and sit with him. But after what had almost happened the previous evening she thought it was wise to not encourage him too much. She wasn't looking for a holiday fling, and if she spent too much time with Ted she might end up doing things with him she shouldn't.

It would be easy to be with him if she wasn't attracted to him. But she was. He was both handsome AND a nice guy. He was also easy to be around.

But she was already in a relationship, all-be-it a difficult one, but this holiday was supposed to give her thinking time and she couldn't do much of that if she was spending all her time with another man.

The sun felt warm on her body and with the hypnotising sound of the waves and the lull of voices mingling around her, Sofia soon found herself falling asleep.

Suddenly she woke up.

How long had she been sleeping?

She opened her eyes and looked around, using her hand to shield her eyes from the sun's glare.

Everything looked the same except that there were a few more people on the beach.

She turned over onto her front and soon found herself drifting off to sleep again.

"Ahh!" The loud yell woke her. Once again she had no idea how long she'd been asleep. She turned over and sat up, looking towards where the noise had come from.

A slim, young woman in a skimpy bikini was being helped out of the water by Ted. He had his arm around her waist and she had both her arms wrapped tightly around his body.

As they came out of the water, Sofia could see a long length of seaweed around one of the young woman's ankles. Ted bent down and unwrapped it then he and the young woman stood looking at it and discussing it before Ted flung it back into the water.

Sofia watched it all with a sinking feeling in her chest. She somehow felt betrayed that Ted was with another woman.

She watched on in further dismay as the young woman picked up her bag and towel as she walked beside Ted and took them to where he'd been sitting. She spread her towel out next to his and the two of them sat together talking and laughing like they were great friends.

Sofia reached into her bag and brought out her book. She opened it and tried to read. But she couldn't fool herself. All she did was place the open book in her lap and tilt her head as though she was reading it, while her eyes looked over at Ted.

Her heart felt like it was breaking as she watched the two of them being so happy together.

The young woman took some food and drink from her bag and shared it with Ted.

Sofia watched them eating together. The two of them seemed so relaxed in each other's company, so far removed from the awkward lunch and evening drink that she'd shared with him the previous day.

Why hadn't she been less uptight with him? She now wished she had been a more fun companion for him.

But why? Why was she wishing that things were different between her and Ted? And why was she so jealous of seeing him with another woman? None of it made sense to her usual oh-so-logical mind.

She sat for a while longer watching the two of them. When they finished their food, they got up and headed back to the water. The young woman took his hand in hers as they waded further out.

Damn they looked so much like a really happy couple.

Sofia lifted her head and stopped pretending to read. She watched Ted laughing and splashing around with his new companion.

Suddenly she saw a familiar figure walking barefoot along the edge of the water. Amy looked up and waved. Sofia waved back. That poor girl was on her own again.

She laid down and tried to concentrate on her book to get her mind off what was going on. But it was difficult.

She soon heard the young woman's voice and glanced over to see her and Ted walking back up the beach, away from the water. Ted looked like he was engrossed in what she was saying and seemed to have forgotten that Sofia was even there at all.

Sofia knew she needed to stop all this jealousy and get back to her book. She took out her bottle of water, drank it all in one go, and then tried to read. But it was no good. Her mind just couldn't rest. And she still had no idea what time it was.

She thought that she should go back to her room in case she'd been out in the sun too long, but she wanted to keep watching Ted, even though it was making her crazy.

She heard the young woman's voice again.

Were they going back for another swim already? But they weren't heading for the water. They were both carrying their belongings and heading off the beach. She heard a snatch of their conversation "Do you want to? Shall we?" the young woman was asking him. "Sure, why not," was Ted's easy answer.

Damn it! Now they had plans together and Sofia had no idea what. Were they going somewhere now? Or were they making plans for tonight?

It didn't really matter. The only thing that was important was that Sofia had missed her chance with Ted.

The only question now, was how was she going to survive the rest of the two-week holiday if she had to endure seeing Ted with someone else?

She had no idea why she should even care about him.

But she did.

Chapter 5. Monday Evening

Sofia had left the beach at what she felt was an appropriate length of time after Ted and the young woman had gone, just to make sure it didn't seem like she was following them.

She didn't have any plans for the rest of the day so she'd stayed inside her room and watched TV and did some beading on the wedding dress she was currently working on.

It should have been a relaxing afternoon, but her mind kept wandering back to Ted and the young woman and she wondered what they were doing.

Later on, after being shut indoors with her thoughts all afternoon, she decided to eat out at one of the local restaurants. It was casual dining in them all and they each had TVs and showed movies and TV shows all day and all evening making it easy to go out and eat and drink alone at any time.

She showered and dressed in a simple yet elegant silver dress and walked out of the resort and along the road. All the bars and restaurants had their menus on stands outside so she browsed them as she went.

Finally she settled on a restaurant that had a few choices of salad and was showing the movie Shirley Valentine about a woman alone in Corfu, which was ironically appropriate.

An enthusiastic Greek waiter showed her to a small table with two chairs. She ordered her food and a glass of wine and felt relaxed for the first time in hours.

Just as she was enjoying her meal, she heard a familiar voice. Glancing at the door she saw Ted and the young woman from the beach with three other young women, all entering together.

The same eager waiter showed them to a table across the other side of the room. When they were all seated, Ted had his back half-turned towards her and he hadn't noticed she was there, so she was able to watch him unseen.

From the way the young women interacted and the way they spoke to each other, it was easy to tell that they were friends holidaying together.

Ted seemed happy in their company and sat laughing and smiling the whole time.

Sofia had that same heavy feeling in her heart that she'd felt earlier at the beach.

She'd felt comfortable in her own company before Ted walked in. Now she felt alone as she watched him enjoying himself surrounded by four, young, female admirers.

Sofia resolved to just ignore them and enjoy her meal and the movie like she'd been doing before the others had walked in.

But her attention keep getting drawn to the table of five. She also started drinking faster and before she knew it, she'd finished her third glass of wine.

Enough was enough. She didn't want to sit here silently eating her heart out any longer.

She motioned the waiter, paid her bill and got up to leave, trying to stride toward the door without Ted seeing her.

Once outside she was tempted to look back and see what he was doing, and whether or not he'd noticed her leave.

But she was immediately distracted by a tall, dark and handsome man sitting at one of the tables outside. "Hey, leaving already?"

Sofia turned to look at him. She hadn't even noticed him until he spoke, but now that she did, she was attracted by his rugged appearance and thick, glossy black hair.

Unsure of how to respond, she asked "Already?"

"I mean before we've been properly introduced. My name's Mario."

"Mario?" she said, sounding surprised.

"Yes. Why?" he asked in his broken English that somehow made him even more attractive.

"Isn't that an Italian name?"

"I am Italian," he stated plainly.

"Oh, I thought you were Greek, with your mediterranean looks and cute accent. Plus we are in Greece." Oh God. Why had she said cute? Now it sounded like she was flirting with him. Why had she had three glasses of wine? Two was her usual limit.

He threw his head back and laughed. She wondered if he knew how beautiful he looked when he did that. "And you are?"

"Sofia."

"Isn't that an Italian name?" he asked, mimicking the way she had asked him.

"Touché. But I'm not from Italy. I'm from England."

"Your parents though...surely they are Italian?"

"My father is."

"Mine too." They both laughed as he continued. "We have so much in common already. Can I buy you a drink?"

She was somewhat taken aback by his forwardness. All she really wanted to do was leave quickly so that Ted wouldn't know that she'd been there. "OK. Yes. I'd like that. But can we go somewhere else?"

"Why?"

"I just feel like a change of scenery."

"Alright. There's a nice little bar further down the street. How about we take a walk together?"

"Sounds perfect."

Mario stood up and together they left the restaurant.

The little bar was simply lit with pleasant music playing in the background and the TV muted which was perfect for people wanting to sit and chat.

Mario went to the bar to get their drinks while Sofia chose a table. She picked a small table for two in the corner of the room where no one passing by would see them.

He came back and sat with her and placed two glasses of white wine on the table.

They sat and talked happily together for what seemed hours while at the same time Sofia was sure that time was flying. They twice ordered another drink each from a roving waiter while they talked.

Eventually Sofia decided it was time to head back to her room. She'd enjoyed her evening with Mario, but she was feeling slightly drunk.

They were both staying at the same resort and Mario's room, it seemed, wasn't too far from hers.

As they headed back along the road, Sofia became even more aware of how much she'd had to drink and for every step she took, she had to make a conscious effort not to stagger.

Mario casually linked arms with her as they walked and she was grateful for the extra stability. He chatted continuously, telling her about the Italian town he lived in. But Sofia was wrapped up in her own thoughts about Ted and the young women, and hoping that she wasn't going to have a hangover the next day.

She reasoned that she couldn't be as drunk as she felt if she was still sober enough to realise she was drunk, and that made perfect sense to her drunken mind.

When they returned to the resort, Mario walked her straight to his room. He stopped outside his door and said, "I have a bottle of gorgeous white wine chilling in the fridge. How about having one more glass with me before our evening ends?"

Sofia shook her head. "Oh no. I've had enough wine. I really need to go home."

"Oh please. Just one glass. It doesn't have to be a big one. I just don't want our time together to end so soon tonight. Please?"

His beautiful smile and pleading expression won her over fast. "Alright. But only one and then I MUST go."

"Fantastic!" He opened his door and they both went inside.

* * * * *

Sofia came awake slowly. Her head hurt and her mouth was dry. She also needed to urinate. Oh God. Why had she drank so much?

As she lay struggling her way to consciousness, she tried to remember exactly what she did the night before.

She remembered the restaurant and Ted walking in with the young women. And then there was Mario and they'd had a few drinks in a quiet bar. She also remembered walking back with him and he'd asked her to have one more drink with him in his room.

She hadn't wanted to but it was so easy to say yes.

And then what?

Her memory was somewhat hazy. She remembered his room being almost identical to hers, and he got wine from the fridge and they sat on his bed and drank it...

Her eyes shot open. Laying there next to her was Mario, still fast asleep.

She was still in his room, tucked up in bed with him.

Oh God! What had she done?

Chapter 6

Tuesday. Day 5

Sofia lay still, just staring at Mario's head on the pillow next to hers. She had no idea how she'd wound up in bed with him, but she wanted to get out of there - fast!

She moved her hands slowly down her body to see what she was wearing, hoping all the time that she wasn't naked. But she seemed to be dressed in the same clothes she'd gone out in the night before.

As slowly as she could, she crept out of bed. Mario lay on his back facing the ceiling, his mouth slightly ajar and breathing deeply.

Sofia quickly looked down. Her dress was severely rumpled and wrinkled from sleeping in it, but at least her shoes were next to the bed in easy reach. She picked them up and looked around for her handbag. Luckily that was in easy reach too, so she picked it up and tiptoed into the kitchen, opened the door on the far side and slipped outside, quietly closing the door behind her.

Then she quickly ran her hands through her hair to straighten it the best she could, slipped on her shoes and made her way back to her own room, hoping she wouldn't see Ted on the way.

Her mind was still groggy from the night before and she was sure that if she was breathalysed, the reading would still be positive.

Families with young children and couples passed her by, all going about their morning business quite happily and sober. She wished she felt that good instead of the heavy, drunken state she was suffering from.

She wondered what time it was. A quick glance at her watch told her it was only 8 am.

As she walked she tried to remember what she and Mario had done in his room. As she concentrated and tried to remember the sequence of events, she briefly remembered kissing him.

They were sat on his bed with a glass of wine each, and he had leaned across and kissed her passionately and held the back of her head with his free hand to prevent her from pulling away.

But she also remembered not wanting to get intimate with him and wanting to pull away.

So what had happened?

Had they been intimate?

Did they have sex?

They had definitely spent the night together. But Sofia was still fully dressed so it was doubtful that they'd had sex.

Why she'd gotten into bed with him, she had no idea. But she was as sure as she could be that they'd not had sex. Or had they?

One thing she was sure of, was that at the moment, with her messy hair and rumpled clothes, she certainly looked like she was doing the early morning walk of shame.

She hesitantly came round the corner to her room, hoping that no one would see her. She didn't look up and no one called her name, so she figured she was safe as she put the key into her lock and slipped into her room.

But what she hadn't seen was Ted coming out of his door at the same time, and the look of hurt on his face when he saw her.

* * * * *

Sofia stayed in her room all day. She didn't want to see anyone.

As soon as she got inside she drank two quick glasses of water, went to the toilet, then showered.

Next she made herself a simple breakfast of baked beans on toast and washed it down with a big glass of orange juice and a cup of coffee.

She felt much better after that, so she put on her nightie and went to bed with the TV on and the sound turned down so that it wasn't loud enough to keep her awake, but it was loud enough to drown out other noises from outside.

By mid afternoon she was awake and felt much better and was hungry again. She made herself a toasted sandwich and a cup of coffee and realised that she was running out of food. Her one and only kitchen cupboard was almost bare. Reluctant as she was to leave her room, she needed supplies otherwise she wouldn't be able to have any more meals in her room.

So she got dressed in shorts and a baggy T-shirt and headed to the small supermarket. She spent some time looking around at all the items they sold, some of which she had no idea what they were.

Eventually she bought what she needed including a bottle of wine and a few beers, so that she could chill out on her own for a few nights if she wanted to.

As she walked back to her room carrying her 3 bags of provisions, she realised that it felt good to be outside again, despite the bad start to the day and her need to hide.

"Hey! Sofia!" She turned and saw Amy walking toward her. Once she caught up with Sofia she walked with her. "I was thinking about going out for dinner tonight but my boyfriend doesn't want to. I've been on my own all day. You don't fancy going out for a bite to eat tonight do you?"

It was perfect timing. Sofia did want to eat out but didn't want to eat alone again. "Actually, yes. I'd love to. I was just thinking about what to do for dinner."

Amy looked really pleased. "Brilliant. How about we meet up out here at about 7 o'clock and go somewhere from there?"

"Sounds good to me. I'll see you at seven."

"See you then." They'd reached Sofia's room so Amy turned and headed to hers.

It felt great to have dinner plans with someone and Amy seemed like such an easy-going and sweet natured person that she was sure they'd have a fun and relaxing meal together.

By 7 o'clock Sofia was showered, dressed and sitting on her patio waiting for Amy, who soon appeared on her own patio. She waved to Sofia and they both met up on the path and walked out of the resort together and along the road toward the restaurants.

They decided to eat at a place where the TV was at the back of the room so it didn't disturb them as they sat at the front.

They both briefly talked about their lives and then Amy told Sofia about how selfish her boyfriend was and that she was using the holiday as the make-or-break deciding factor as to whether or not she should stay with him, and so far he was being more selfish than usual so Amy had grave doubts about their future together. Their situation was also complicated by the fact that they lived together so if Amy left him, she'd also lose her home.

Sofia told her that she too was in a similar position with her boyfriend, Jason, only she didn't live with him and she'd left him behind so that she could think. She also told Amy about her Ted and Mario problem too and about the cute blonde pursuing Ted.

Amy listened intently, asking questions now and then and finally saying, "Wow. You really have got a complicated situation."

Sofia laughed. "This was supposed to be a quiet, stress-free holiday with nothing to do but think. And I'm still not sure how it changed so completely."

"I'd say forget everything and go after Ted. I can tell that he's the one you really want to be with. And if he doesn't know about Mario, then you haven't messed things up with him, regardless of whether you and the Italian Stallion bumped uglies or not." Sofia laughed out loud at Amy's astuteness, honesty and funny way of saying "had sex."

But at the same time, what Amy said struck a chord. Sofia knew that if she was completely honest with herself, Ted was the man she wanted to be with. She wondered if she would have had a relationship with him if she'd been single. But what would be the point? They were only here for two weeks and they lived over 100 miles apart back home in the UK, so there really was no reason to even think about it.

She and Amy enjoyed their meal together and laughed a lot. Sofia drank orange juice with her dinner and had a coffee afterwards still conscious of how much she'd had to drink the night before and thought her body (and mind) could do with less alcohol.

"Tell me Sofia, what do you think I should do? Love him or leave him?"

"It's not my place to give you advice. I don't even know your boyfriend."

"You don't have to. You only need to know how he makes me feel."

"Well in that case, it's easy to see that he makes you feel sad and lonely. I mean here you are on holiday together and it's the perfect opportunity to spend some intimate time together and instead he wants to spend time AWAY from you. And that's from the little bit I know and have seen."

Amy slumped in her chair and looked thoughtful for a few moments. "You're right. He doesn't make me happy at all anymore. Even here where there's nothing to do, he still doesn't want to be with me."

Sofia felt bad for voicing her opinion. "Amy don't pay any attention to me. I shouldn't have said anything. Who am I to talk about other people's relationships when I can't even sort out my own?"

Amy suddenly sat forward and smiled. "I'll tell you what. Seeing as we're both at a crossroad in our relationships, you tell me what you think I should do and I'll tell you what I think you should do. Not that it matters," she continued, holding up the palm of her hand towards Sofia. "We're both here on holiday, we both have boyfriend problems, so it wouldn't hurt to get a second opinion."

Sofia loved Amy's simple logic, and it made sense. "Alright, let's do it. But we mustn't hold each other accountable if we follow their advice and it all goes wrong."

"Deal," said Amy. "You first."

"OK. I think that you are extremely unhappy in your relationship. You don't want the stress and hassle of breaking up and moving out but it's what you really want to do, otherwise you wouldn't even be thinking about it.

"You came here on holiday as a last-ditch effort to change things, hoping it would be different here. But it's not. All it's done is confirm what you already know. It will never be different. It's over. You need to enjoy yourself without him while you're here and then end things once and for all when you get home."

Amy sat and stared at Sofia while she was speaking. After a few seconds she responded. "Wow. It's like you can see straight into my mind. I've never thought about it like that but you're right in everything you said. I have been limping this relationship along for longer than I should. And you're also right that nothing is going to change. Coming here has even somehow made it worse. It's over. I can see it now."

"Amy, I'm sorry."

"No, don't be. I'm not. Hearing you sum it all up like that has made everything so much clearer. I can see now how much I've been deluding myself into thinking that if I just hang on long enough, things will change and it will all be good again. Talk about eye-opening. This is amazing."

"I didn't want to make you feel bad."

"No, no. You didn't. If anything I feel stronger. I've never had such clarity about it before. I will end it as soon as I get home because I deserve better than him. Being alone is even preferable to being with someone who doesn't care about you."

Sofia was amazed and happy about Amy's strong resolve.

"Now I'll do you," Amy said enthusiastically. "And I hope it gives you as much clarity too."

"OK. Hit me with your insight."

Amy took a big breath. "Well, for starters, your relationship with your boyfriend is a no-go zone. It seems that he has absolutely no respect for you and belittles everything you do. Usually people do that for one of two reasons. Either they're jealous or they're manipulating you to try and make you feel inferior to them. Either way, you don't need him. Even the fact that you had to leave the country to get away from him speaks volumes.

"Next is your Ted-blonde chick-Mario situation. I say go for everything with Ted. He's the one you've been attracted to since the moment you met him. Just forget Mario. He was a mistake. We all make them. And fight for Ted. Screw the little blonde chick. I don't think he wants to be with her anyway. Even when he went out for dinner with her they weren't alone. She had all her friends tagging long with her so it was hardly a romantic dinner for two.

"And even if they did go back to his room and do the uglies, so what? You spent the night with the Italian Stallion. So touché. Forget it and move on.

"If you want to be with Ted just do it and stop overthinking everything because I can tell that you do. Maybe you and Ted will get together once you're home and maybe you won't. But at least you'll have fond memories of being with him here. Don't pass up the opportunity, otherwise you'll spend the rest of your life wondering 'what if?'"

It was Sofia's turn to be amazed. Amy had certainly grasped Sofia's situation and, as much as she didn't want to admit it, she was right about needing to end her relationship with Jason as soon as she got home.

"Well that certainly is clarity about my situation. I DO need to end things with my boyfriend and you're also right about his complete lack of respect for me.'

Amy smiled and clapped her hands together. "I knew it! And what about Ted? Are you going to go for broke?"

"I have wanted to be with him all the time and it crushed me seeing him with someone else. But I don't know if I want to have a clíched 'holiday fling.' I don't want to do that."

"Sure you do," said Amy confidently.

Sofia thought about it. "It's not so much the fling, it's the regrets of doing it that I might have to live with for the rest of my life."

"Oh phooey," said Amy dismissively. "He's handsome, you're gorgeous, you both want each other, what's to regret?"

Both women laughed at Amy's simple logic.

"One thing is for sure," said Sofia. "Both you and I have some breaking up to do when we get home."

After dinner Sofia and Amy walked back to their rooms together. As they stood outside on the grass to say goodbye, Amy said, "Well I wish you luck and hope you get your man."

"I wish you luck too and I hope you can enjoy the rest of your holiday now that your mind is made up."

"You bet I will. Every day I try and persuade him to come and do something with me and he keeps saying no. But now that I don't care it will be easier to just do what I want every day without feeling that I have to explain where I'm going and begging him to come too."

"Sounds like a plan."

"Yeah. And it's a good one too. Thanks for all your insightful help tonight. I really feel so much better about everything."

"So do I. Thanks for your insights too."

"Just go and get your new man," said Amy with a smirk.

"Goodnight."

"Goodnight Sofia," and with that Amy turned and headed to her own room.

Sofia went in through her kitchen door and walked straight ahead to the patio door in the bedroom, throwing down her bag and keys as she went and switching on the lights.

Opening the door she stepped outside and almost immediately Lenore appeared from around the dividing wall. "There you are Sofia. We were wondering where you got to tonight. Come and have a drink with us." Without waiting for an answer, she turned and disappeared again.

Sofia had been looking forward to sitting out and having a bit of a quiet time on her own, but she thought "Why not? I'm only here for a few days and I can spend as many evenings on my own as I want once I'm home." So she pulled her door almost shut and went around the wall.

There at the table were Lenore, Mick and Ted. Sofia was taken off-guard to see Ted there too.

"Sofia," said Mick with a quick nod.

Ted only gave her a quick smile and then looked out over the garden as though he was mesmerised with the view.

"Wine?" asked Lenore as she got up and went inside.

"Thanks," smiled Sofia, somewhat amused at Lenore's habit of always assuming an answer to her question before she received a response.

Lenore quickly came back with the drink and put it in front of Sofia before sitting back down in her own chair.

"Thanks." Sofia picked up the glass and took a quick sip to avoid having to look at Ted. It just felt so awkward to be with him when she didn't know how he felt about the cute blonde and she still felt guilty about Mario. Plus Ted seemed like he didn't want to talk to her. It was the first time she'd seen him without his permanent smile.

Lenore suddenly interrupted her thoughts. "Have you had a good evening?"

"Yes. I had a meal at a really nice restaurant, but I can't remember the name of it."

"Who did you have dinner with?" That question was from Mick.

Lenore responded before Sofia had a chance. "Mick, don't be so rude. It's none of our business who Sofia had a date with."

"I was only asking."

"Well if she wanted us to know, she'd have said."

Mick shrugged. Lenore apologised to Sofia. "Sorry Sofia."

"Don't you speak for me. If I want to say sorry to someone I can do it myself. But I only asked a simple question," said Mick in his usual soft manner.

Lenore glared at him. "Let's drop it shall we?"

Mick shrugged again. Sofia cut in before Lenore could say anything else. "It wasn't a date as such. I had dinner with a woman who's staying in a room over there." She pointed past her own room.

"Hey Ted!" They all looked up at the sound of the voice. The cute blonde was coming across the lawn towards then. "Can I have a word with you?"

"Sure," said Ted not moving from his chair.

"In private?" She asked half turning away as though she was about to walk away but wanted Ted to follow.

Ted obediently stood up and followed her. The two of them disappeared around the corner of the building.

"Looks like he's got an admirer there, lucky devil," said Mick.

"Don't be so presumptuous." This from Lenore. "They're probably just friends like Sofia and the woman she had dinner with."

Mick sighed. "I was just saying."

"Well don't!" she snapped.

Sofia had no idea why Lenore was being so bad tempered with Mick. But with their raised voices that she'd heard through her wall many times, it seemed that Lenore was always angry with him. Goodness knew how or why Mick put up with it.

But now it was making her really uncomfortable and coupled with the fact that Ted had disappeared with the cute blonde, left her feeling even more miserable. She wished she hadn't sat down with them at all.

Suddenly Ted appeared again, walking back around the corner of the building. The cute blonde was still with him.

Ted stepped back up onto the patio and the cute blonde headed away with a loud and over-exuberant, "See you later, Ted." Ted gave her a quick wave then took a drink from his bottle of beer.

"Who's your friend?" Sofia hoped it sounded like a casual question when in reality she was dying to know what was happening between the two of them.

Ted seemed happy to explain. "That's Caroline. I met her on the beach the other day and then she stuck to me like glue, even taking me back to her room to meet her friends and then insisting that we all go out to dinner together.

"At first I thought 'why not?' but she's turned out to be really clingy and needy and no matter how many times I tell her that I don't want to swim with her or hang out with her or have lunch with her, she just keeps on asking. I thought she would have got the message by now but as you saw, she keeps on tracking me down."

Ted's expression suddenly changed and he looked seriously at Sofia. "In fact, last night when I was with her and her friends at the restaurant, I wanted to leave early and have a drink with you. But as I got up to leave, I saw you disappear out of the restaurant with another guy. I didn't even know you were there until then.

" So I came back here and waited for you to come home, but you never did so eventually I went to bed."

Sofia felt terrible. She had no idea that Ted had seen her that night or that he wanted to be with her. She certainly would have preferred his company to Mario's.

She quickly tried to make light of the situation. "Oh him? He was more into himself than into any woman. Turned out to be quite a bore. And I don't know why you didn't see me come back that night. Maybe we were both tired."

She hated lying to him, and the whole situation of Ted and the cute blonde, herself and Mario, and Lenore's constant criticism of Mick just exhausted her.

So far this holiday was far removed from the stress-free, quiet time she'd been expecting.

She wondered just how awkward this whole thing could get.

Little did she know she was about to find out.

Chapter 7

Wednesday Morning. Day 6

Sofia sat out on her patio eating breakfast. It was only 7.30 but she'd gotten up early because she couldn't sleep. The whole Ted and Mario thing kept going around in her head. She wondered if she'd ever stop feeling guilty about spending the night with Mario. And she wasn't even sure why she felt so guilty. After all, she and Ted weren't a couple and she was still almost sure that she hadn't had sex with Mario anyway.

As she thought about it she realised that she wasn't feeling bad about it because of Ted (although that did add to her guilt), but because she was disappointed in herself. She should never have gotten so drunk and definitely should not have gone back to his room with him.

At the time she'd kept telling herself that it wouldn't hurt to have just one more drink with him. But on reflection, she realised she had allowed herself to be manipulated, plus there was only one reason a guy like him would want to take a woman into his room late at night, and that was for sex.

How could she have been so naive and so gullible?

Obviously the answer was the alcohol. She'd simply had too much. Well, if nothing else it was a lesson learned, never EVER have so much to drink in one evening.

Sofia got up and took her breakfast dishes into the kitchen. She washed and dried them and put them away and then made herself another cup of coffee before heading back out to the patio with it. She turned on the TV as she went, tuned it to a local radio station and picked up her sewing.

Once back outside she settled down and took out the wedding dress bodice and the jar of tiny silver beads and started sewing. It felt really relaxing just sitting and working on a warm morning with the music playing unobtrusively in the background. This was how her holiday should have been all along.

As she sat and sewed, other people began to emerge from their rooms. She kept glancing up and watching them as they began their day.

After a while she went inside to see what time it was. According to the bedside alarm clock it was five past ten. She must have been sitting on the patio longer than she thought.

She went to the kitchen for a glass of juice and took it back outside. Once again she picked up the dress bodice and continued beading it.

"Sofia!" She cringed at the familiar voice.

Looking up from her work she said, "Hi Mario."

Without waiting for an invitation he stepped up and sat in the empty chair at her table.

"You snuck out on me the other morning."

Oh no. He was acting as though they were a couple. She looked down at her work and resumed beading as she spoke. "I just left. You were snoring so you probably didn't hear me. "She knew it was a lie but he wouldn't know if he was snoring or not.

"It would have been amazing to wake up next to you. I was disappointed that you were gone."

Sofia inwardly cringed, imagining how awful it would have been if he'd have woken up first and touched her while she slept. She didn't know what to say.

At that moment someone else appeared at the edge of her patio. Looking up she saw it was Ted. He was looking at Mario, and Sofia felt her heart physically sink in her chest.

"Oh hi, Ted." she said quickly to break the sudden awkward silence. Perhaps she could use him as an excuse to get rid of Mario. "Would you like a coffee?"

She half rose from her chair as she spoke but Ted put his hand up to stop her. "No need. I was just heading out for breakfast and wondered if you wanted to join me, but I can see you're busy." His head slightly jerked towards Mario as he said the last two words.

Sofia was about to say "Oh, I'd love to. Sorry Mario I have to go." But before she could say anything, Ted turned and disappeared from sight behind the dividing wall.

Having a solid wall to separate the patios was a good thing but it meant that she couldn't see where people went if they walked in that direction.

What she really wanted to do was run after Ted and explain, but by the hurt and angry look on his face he probably wouldn't have believed her anyway. It must have looked to him as though she and Mario were having a cosy chat together, even though the opposite was true. He'd only just arrived and Sofia was trying to get rid of him.

"You know...you owe me another evening together." Sofia couldn't believe what she was hearing. As far as she was concerned she owed him nothing. "We already had an evening together."

"Yes but it was cut short by how much we'd had to drink and how tired you were. You fell asleep so fast and I put the covers over you and looked after you.

"I was thinking that we could start fresh this evening and this time finish what we started in the bedroom," he said, with a slow wink.

Sofia felt a rush of relief. If Mario wanted to finish what they started then it meant they hadn't had sex at all. Thank goodness! Now all she had to do was get rid of him once and for all, without upsetting him or making him angry.

"Look...I don't want to mess you around. We're all here on a short holiday and if you're looking for a fling while you're here, then you're looking in the wrong place."

"You see, I'm not looking to hook up with anyone. I'm not even looking for a one night stand. I'm only here for a quiet time and a chance to do nothing at all. I'm sorry but like I said, I don't want to waste your time."

But Mario obviously wasn't prepared to let her go that easily. "But look at how far we've already come and all that we have in common with both of us having Italian heritage. All I'm asking is for one dinner together. Tonight."

"But you said that the evening will finish in your room, not the restaurant, and I told you, I'm not looking for that."

"Why? What's wrong with you?"

"I just don't like sex to be an obligation."

"It won't be."

"Yes it will. You said you want us to finish what we started the other night."

"I just meant kissing and passionate embraces. I was kind to you the other night when you were really drunk."

"And now I'm obligated to you?"

"Not at all." Mario was getting angry. "I just came here to invite you to dinner and you're twisting my words."

"No. You said you wanted to take me back to your room. That's not dinner."

"Why are you making such a big deal of this?"

"Why are you still here? I keep saying no, but you keep insisting. So here it is again. No!"

Mario feigned confusion. "I don't know why you're acting this way."

Sofia sighed heavily. "What I really want to do is get away from you, but you won't leave."

"You think I'm some kind of monster that you have to run away from? You have some serious insecurity issues."

Sofia felt angry and didn't try to hide it anymore. "Will you just LEAVE."

Mario stood up abruptly, his chair scraping back loudly across the floor. "Don't worry. I don't want to be around a woman like you who has so many issues. You need to get over your mistrust of men." And with that he stepped off her patio and strode away across the grass.

Sofia stood up and took one last parting shot at him. "It's not all men I mistrust. I just don't want to be with you!"

She picked up her belongings from the table, took them inside and closed and locked the door. Normally she didn't lock it through the day time when she was in, but she didn't trust Mario.

She found a TV channel showing an old movie and sat down and tried to carry on beading while she watched it.

But the distraction didn't work. All she could think about was Ted and she wondered where he was and what he was thinking.

After a while she put her sewing away and turned off the TV because she couldn't concentrate on either.

She lay on the bed and stared at the ceiling. It was time for some rational thinking.

The one thing she was sure of was that she didn't ever want to even speak to Mario ever again. So if she ran into him again, she'd be polite (because she didn't want to make a scene) but be completely aloof. And that would solve the Mario issue.

But what about Ted? First he had waited up for her but she hadn't come home. Then she lied to him and said that she had come home late that night. She hadn't told him the truth and that she'd spent the night with Mario. She could never tell him that. He didn't need to know because nothing sexual had happened and knowing she'd spent the night with another man would only hurt him.

The other issue was the cute blonde. But Ted had said that he wasn't interested in her and she believed him.

But the cute blonde was obviously interested in Ted because she turned up at his room last night while they were all sat out having a drink together. No doubt she'd been hoping to find him alone.

But what if Ted became interested in her now that he'd seen Sofia sat with Mario?

Oh good grief! She couldn't believe the childishness of her thoughts. "He likes me but she likes him..." How ridiculous was that?

She was sick of feeling like a jealous school girl. Amy had been right. She did want to be with Ted.

But why did she? This was just a two week holiday and so far, in less than one week, she'd slept with one man while wanting to be with another man who was being pursued by another woman.

How did this whole thing get so complicated?

Suddenly, she had an epiphany.

What she needed to do was stop letting it be so complicated. She had to do what she wanted to do and stop trying to control the outcome.

What she needed to do was go and find Ted and explain why Mario was sitting with her and how she didn't want to but he wouldn't leave.

Yes. That was it. Just do what she felt must be done and let the rest of it take care of itself.

But where was Ted? He said he was going out for breakfast so maybe he was back.

Sofia grabbed her keys and went to Ted's room. She knocked twice but there was no answer, so she headed out to the local restaurants and bars to see if he was still there.

Then a thought struck her. What if she found him having breakfast with the cute blonde, Caroline? Ted said her name was Caroline. She must stop thinking of her as the cute blonde.

So what if she did find him with Caroline? What would she say?

She'd still do the same. She'd tell Ted that Mario was a pest she couldn't get rid of. And if he asked why she was telling him, she'd say because she'd offered him a cup of coffee as a way to be able to ask Mario to leave..."Sorry Mario. I just need to have a word or two with my friend. You don't mind, do you?" And he would have gone. She just needed to pretend that she'd found Ted by accident and was just imparting some clarity on the previous, uncomfortable situation.

But Ted wasn't in any of the bars or restaurants nor was he in the supermarket or the souvenir shop.

So she tried the bars and eateries at the resort, and then the pool and then she walked up and down the beach. But Ted seemed to be nowhere. But she did see Amy standing alone, knee deep in the water staring across at the mainland of Greece. Poor Amy.

But now what should she do about Ted?

Suddenly it occurred to her that she hadn't seen Caroline either. Were they together somewhere? But where? She'd searched everywhere she could think of, including Ted's room.

But she hadn't tried Caroline's room, and she couldn't because she didn't know which one it was.

So she began a tour of walking through the garden areas, weaving her way through all the rows of rooms, glancing at every patio to see if Ted and Caroline were there.

But she still couldn't find him. Maybe she'd simply missed him. Maybe as she moved from one place to another so did he, so that they were always in a different place to each other.

Or maybe, just maybe, he wasn't in any of the places she'd looked. Maybe he was in Caroline's room with her and that's why she hadn't seen him sitting outside with her.

Many of the rooms she'd passed had their doors and curtains closed as though no one was there. But maybe they were. Sofia herself had sat in her room with the doors and curtains closed the other day.

The thought of Ted and Caroline together in bed made her miserable. She just hoped she was wrong.

But what if she was right?

Chapter 8

Wednesday. Midday. Day 6

Sofia ended her search for Ted and Caroline, or perhaps she should think of it as her search for Ted on his own. She didn't want to associate him with Caroline as though they were a couple, even if it was only in her own mind.

So where Ted was she had no idea. But she was close to her own room so she headed there.

The end patio in her row, Ted's, was empty. Then Lenore and Mick's patio came into view, and before she saw them she knew they were sitting outside because she heard Lenore's loud laugh.

Then she saw that Ted was sitting with them.

Had he been there the whole time? As she left via her kitchen door at the other side of the building, had he already been there? She had no idea. But the empty plates in front of them on the table told her that they'd had a meal together.

"Hey Sofia. There you are," smiled Lenore. "We were looking for you earlier to see if you wanted to join us for lunch. Come and have a drink with us. We're just about to crack open a few cold beers."

Sofia didn't really want a beer but she did want to be with Ted so she said, "Sure. Why Not? Thanks," as she stepped up onto the patio and took a seat with them.

Lenore stacked the dirty plates and cutlery and took them inside as she went.

Ted stared off into the garden, avoiding eye contact with Sofia, so she turned to Mick. "What did you have for lunch?"

"It was a takeaway pizza. Lenore sent me out to get it."

Just then Lenore appeared with four small bottles of beer and put them on the table. "Don't say it like that. I didn't force you to go and get it. I ordered it and you went to pick it up."

"You told me to go and get it."

"But I didn't MAKE you."

"I didn't say you did. I just said you sent me."

Lenore sighed as though she was dealing with a difficult child. "OK. Whatever. Just stop trying to make me out as the bad person. We had a takeaway pizza. That's all you had to say."

"Fine." Mick looked sullenly at the table.

Sofia opened one of the bottles and took a drink from it. Lenore's attitude to Mick made her extremely uncomfortable.

She looked at Ted, but he was staring at his beer and completely ignoring her. But he didn't look angry. He looked upset.

Sofia changed the subject and hoped to get Ted's attention at the same time. "I had a close encounter of the ugly kind this morning and I thought Ted was going to rescue me but he didn't."

Ted looked up at her curiously, but his usual smile still wasn't there, so she continued.

"I had a drink with an Italian guy a couple of nights ago and this morning he appeared unexpectedly and was trying to pressure me into going out to dinner with him.

"Then Ted suddenly appears and I thought he'd come to rescue me but instead he left me so I ended up having to give a stern rejection and got a really angry response from the guy."

She turned to look directly at Ted, who now seemed interested in what she had to say.

"I thought you might have recognised an uncomfortable situation after the trouble you've been having with Caroline. If it happens again, don't leave. Believe me, you won't be interrupting anything."

Ted responded but still wasn't smiling. "He was sitting with you so early in the morning that I wasn't sure if he'd been there all night."

"Well thanks for that," said Sofia, trying to make a joke, but failing. "So you think I'd jump into bed with a guy I'd just met?"

"I don't know," he said, looking straight into her eyes. Sofia was stunned and didn't know what to say. But Ted had a point. They really didn't know each other yet, having only met less than a week ago.

Was it really only a few days? So much had happened that it seemed like much longer.

In fact, this whole holiday was feeling somewhat surreal. It was as though she'd jumped out of her old life and had landed in this new one, and was going to stay here forever.

But it wasn't a new life. It was just a two week vacation, and as Ted had just pointed out, they hardly knew each other at all.

But she felt that she knew Ted enough to like him and she didn't want to lose him as a friend. She wanted to see more of him while she was there, although why, she wasn't sure.

This holiday really did feel like a whole new life.

Chapter 9

Wednesday Afternoon. Day 6

After having a lunch-time drink with Lenore, Mick and Ted, Sofia went back to her room.

She sat on her patio and continued to bead the bodice of the wedding dress she was making, while she thought about Ted.

In her mind she relived their meeting at the airport, their time spent with Lenore and Mick, their happy trip to Corfu Town, and how jealous she felt when she saw him with Caroline.

But why was she obsessing over Ted?

Could it be because she was unhappy with Jason.

When she'd left, she'd told Jason that the two weeks she was gone would give them both time to decide whether or not they wanted to continue their relationship.

And now she sat here wondering if this feeling of living a whole new life here was because she had always subconsciously wanted a whole new life away from Jason?

Being so far away from him meant that she had two weeks away from arguments and snide remarks.

But not just from him.

No one in her family had any respect for anything Sofia did.

Her parents were obsessed with money and were always interested when Sofia was married and both she and her husband had plenty of money.

But they couldn't care less about her bridal gown business, and instead would lavish attention on Sofia's older sister and talk about her job in the bank.

For some reason (that Sofia could never work out) her parents seemed to consider working in a bank as an elite position.

Being in Corfu was far removed from Sofia's usual life and she loved it.

The locals were all extremely friendly even though they obviously didn't have much money, and being around her new friends, there was no judgement. In fact, they never even discussed what they did for a living.

They all took each other at face value and Sofia loved that.

With that thought she resolved to make the best of things while she was here and with what little time they had left.

And with her sudden resolve, Sofia put away her sewing and walked purposefully to Ted's patio.

He was sat at his table reading a book. He looked up as she approached and seemed both surprised and pleased to see her.

Then she did something that she'd never done before. She asked him to dinner. Never in her life had she asked a man for a date.

Without hesitation, Ted accepted, and he said he'd meet her at 7 o'clock.

Sofia felt both relieved and elated.

Chapter 10

Wednesday Evening. Day 6

Ted was extremely punctual and arrived at 7 o'clock on the dot. Sofia wondered if he'd sat staring at his watch for a few minutes before arriving, to time it so precisely.

He was his usual, smiling self again and Sofia was glad. She'd wondered if their evening together was going to be as tense as their lunch-time drinks had been.

They dined in one of the local restaurants and chose a table outside on the large wooden veranda.

Ted ordered a bottle of wine.

While they ate, they both kept the conversation light, discussing their holiday and how much they liked Corfu.

After they finished eating Ted poured them each another glass of wine, sat back thoughtfully for a few seconds, and then said, "I want to get this out in the open so I'm just going to say it."

Sofia felt her whole body stiffen in apprehension. She had no idea what Ted was going to say, but his tone was deadly serious.

Ted stared at his wine glass as he said, "I know that you said that the Italian guy had only just arrived on your patio that morning, but I know that you did spend the night with him a few nights before that."

Sofia felt her heart start pounding loudly in her chest as though it was going to break. At the same time her mind whirled.

How did Ted know? Had he followed her? Had he seen how drunk she was that night?

She didn't know what to say, so she stayed quiet.

Eventually, Ted pulled his gaze away from his wine glass and looked at her. "I waited up for you that night. I wanted to talk to you. I'd seen you leave the bar that night with the Italian guy, but you didn't come home.

"The next morning I saw you sneaking back to your place wearing the same clothes from the night before. I could tell you'd just woken up. I knew where you'd been." He sounded sad as he spoke the last sentence.

Sofia looked down at her wine glass and turned the stem around and around with her fingers as she thought about what to say.

Finally she looked up at him. "You're right and you're wrong. I ran into him that night and he asked if I wanted to have a drink with him. I said yes because I saw you with Caroline, and I'd already had a couple of drinks with my dinner.

"Then one drink with him turned into two or three, I can't remember exactly, but I was drunk by that time. He asked me back to his room for another drink and I'd had so many drinks that the thought of having another seemed like a bloody good idea.

"But I think we'd both drank too much and I think we both fell asleep before we'd even finished that last drink. Anyway, I woke up early and snuck out before he woke up. I knew that by then my dress was all rumpled and my hair was a mess and anyone who saw me would think I was doing the walk-of-shame. But it was just the I-fell-asleep-drunk walk and I showered and then slept the morning away. I had no idea you'd seen me."

To Sofia's surprise, Ted grinned. She'd wondered if he'd believe her story or not, but he obviously did because he smiled and said, "Yeah, your dress was pretty rumpled. I could tell you'd slept in it."

Sofia laughed. "I am never going to drink that much again. I don't know what was worse; sleeping uncomfortably in my clothes or the raging hangover the next morning. Or both. Plus I kind of missed a day of my holiday because I needed to sleep it off till I felt human again."

Ted seemed happy with her confession of what had actually happened. Thank goodness Mario had told her that they hadn't had sex, because for a while she wasn't sure, although she always suspected that they hadn't. But it was a warning not to drink too much while in a foreign country amongst strangers.

Sofia was so relieved that Ted believed her and that he was with her again. The last day or two without him had been somewhat sad days.

She really wasn't sure why she cared about him so much, seeing as they'd only just met, but she did. So perhaps the best thing to do was to relax and simply let things happen.

Trust to fate.

They happily chatted as they finished the bottle of wine, and then walked slowly back to their rooms together.

Ted asked her, "Do you fancy another drink once we get back, or have you had too much already?"

"Oh, ha ha," she responded, playfully punching him on the arm. "Are you going to never let that go?"

Ted laughed. "Yeah, but I couldn't resist taking at least one good shot."

They went back to Ted's room. Sofia sat at the table on the patio while Ted went inside. He came back with two open bottles of beer and put one down in front of Sofia.

At the same time Lenore and Mick arrived. They too had been out for the evening and had just arrived back.

Lenore was in high spirits. "Mind if we join you? Mick, go and get a couple of chairs and some beers."

Obediently, Mick turned and headed back to their room and returned swiftly with two plastic patio chairs and a couple of beers. They all moved around to fit all four chairs around the small table.

"So," said Lenore, "what have you two been up to tonight?"

Ted replied, "We went out for dinner."

"Together?" Enquired Lenore. "Like a date?"

"Like a dinner," Ted told her flatly, hinting that he didn't want to answer her question.

But Lenore either didn't take the hint or chose to ignore it. "Are you guys an item now? Have you kissed and made up?"

Mick quickly interrupted her. "It's not our business. They just had dinner. Leave it alone."

"Yes it is our business. We're friends aren't we? Ted just tell me if I'm interfering."

"You're interfering," he said quickly.

"Told you, " said Mick, quietly.

Lenore shot him an angry look that said, "We'll discuss this later."

To Ted and Sofia she smilingly said, "So, any occasion to celebrate, or just a quiet meal?"

Ted laughed, "We're on holiday. We eat out all the time. It's no big deal."

"Oh poo," said Lenore, pretending to sulk. "I need a bit of gossip. Everyone here is on just an innocent vacation. There's nothing juicy happening."

"Where did you go this evening?" Ted asked her, and so the usual chit chat began between the four of them. To Sofia, it felt as though they were all old friends.

When they'd finished their beers, Lenore wanted to have another one, but Mick persuaded her to go back to their room with him. Sofia was grateful because she wanted to end the night alone with Ted, for what reason she didn't know, but it just felt right.

As soon as Lenore and Mick were gone, Ted quietly said, "Finally, we're alone. Want another drink?"

"With you? Absolutely," Sofia smiled at him.

Ted returned her smile and headed back inside for two more drinks.

When he came back he placed the bottles on the table and pulled his chair up to hers. Then he casually put his arm around her. Sofia was pleasantly surprised but at the same time curious as to what he would do next.

But she didn't have to wait long.

He picked up his beer, leaned the bottle towards hers as he said, "Cheers." She picked up her bottle and tapped it on his. "Cheers."

After they both took a sip and placed their bottles back on the table, Ted turned to her, put his finger under her chin to tilt her head towards his, and kissed her.

It was a lingering kiss, and she loved it, while at the same time wanting to pull away because she knew it was wrong, even though it felt so right.

As they kissed, Ted put his hand on her thigh. She was wearing a short skirt, so his hand touched her flesh.

She responded by placing a hand on his thigh, although he was wearing long, cotton pants, but she felt his leg stiffen through the material.

Ted's hand left her thigh and cupped her breast through her blouse. She let out a small, involuntary moan of pleasure.

His kiss, his breath, his touch, all felt so amazing. She wanted to abandon herself to him, but she was thinking that it was wrong. She was still in a relationship with Jason. She shouldn't be intimate with another man.

And what about Ted? He was only recently divorced and was probably on the rebound, looking for quick and easy sex. That could be the reason he came here and why he set his sights on Sofia right from the start.

They really shouldn't be doing what they were doing. It wasn't right. But now Ted's hand was inside her bra, massaging her breast.

He moved his lips to her neck and mouthed her skin, while his other hand caressed her upper thigh under her skirt.

It was all so wrong and yet so good. She couldn't think fast enough because it was all happening so quickly and she was loving every second of it, and responding intimately.

One of her hands was up the back of his shirt, caressing his flesh, while the other moved up his thigh and cupped the bulge in his crotch.

Ted suddenly let out a quiet moan of pleasure, then he stood up, took Sofia by the hand, and led her inside, locking the door behind them.

Her mind screamed at her. "What are you doing? He's probably only looking for a quickie!"

But as Ted began to undress her, and kiss and mouth her flesh as he did so, she thought, "I have no idea where this is going to lead in the future, but right now I want to be here and I want to do this. I want to be naked with Ted and I want to have sex with him. It might be the wrong thing to do, but right now it's what I want to do. I'll deal with the consequences later."

And with that, she began to undress him, kissing and touching every part of his body as she did so, and she shivered with desire even more as their naked bodies pressed together and his lips met hers once more.

Even though she knew what she was doing was wrong, it felt so right. Being intimate with Ted was somehow better than anything she'd ever had with another man. She knew she'd never felt this way before.

Afterwards, while they lay naked in bed together, she knew that no matter what, even if she never saw Ted again once they left the island, she would always remember this night and would never regret it.

And now, laying naked in his arms while feeling herself drifting to sleep, felt like paradise. It was a feeling she'd never felt before.

Chapter 11

Thursday Morning. Day 7

Sofia awoke the next morning feeling slightly guilty.

She'd woken in the early hours of the morning in Ted's room, gathered her clothes from where they'd been scattered all over the floor, put on her skirt and blouse, kept her underwear in her hand, kissed Ted on the cheek (who woke slightly and mumbled, "don't go"), and went back to her own room.

She hadn't wanted the awkwardness of waking up together after having sex for the first time the night before, especially as she'd only known him for a few days.

She showered and dressed as she relived the previous evening and resolved to not pressure Ted into being with her if he didn't want to, just in case she was right and he was on the rebound after being recently divorced.

And as for Jason, well, she really didn't know.

How could she be with him after being with another man? AND if she really wanted to be with him, would she have slept with someone else?

Deep down she knew that Amy had been completely correct a few days ago when she'd said that Sofia didn't want to be with Jason at all anymore.

If she was honest with herself, what she really wanted was for this life in Corfu to never end and she and Ted to be a couple forever. But she knew that could never really happen.

She saw her mobile phone on her bedside table. She'd had it with her the whole time she'd been here, but hadn't switched it on because she didn't want to talk to anyone while she was away, and instead wanted to completely immerse herself in her time here.

She wondered if Jason had been trying to contact her. Just out of curiosity, she turned on her phone.

She saw that there were several unread messages and a missed call from Jason.

Before she'd left, she told him that she would be turning her phone off while she was away so that they could have a complete break and time to think.

Looking at those missed messages and the phone call from him felt strange. It was as though her old life was trying to intrude on her new life. Yet what now seemed like her old life, was actually her real life.

Right now, sitting in her room here in Corfu, it felt like this was where she now belonged, here with Ted and Lenore and Mick and Amy.

Back in Bath, England was her real life where her family and friends were, and her handmade, bridal gown business. She knew it was true but she didn't want to think about it.

She switched off her phone again. She didn't want to read the unopened messages because she really didn't want to know what he had to say.

Sitting on the edge of her bed and staring at the blank screen of her phone, she couldn't even imagine what it would be like to see Jason again, and she wasn't sure if she wanted to either. Regardless of what would happen between her and Ted, she didn't want to have anything to do with Jason.

But now was not the time to think about it. She was only half-way through her holiday and had another week to stay in Corfu, so she would make the best of things while she was here, enjoy the weather, spend time with her new friends and let the future take care of itself.

She felt happy with her new resolve to just enjoy herself while she was here and forget about everything else. After all, that's what vacations are for, aren't they? To get away from life for a while?

Well, today was another gorgeous, sunny day so after enjoying a quiet cup of coffee and a couple of slices of toast in her room while catching up with the news on TV, she changed into her bikini, put a loose cotton dress over the top, put a few things in her tote bag, slipped on a pair of sandals, and headed off to the pool.

She spread her towel on an empty poolside lounge chair, put her bag on top, slipped off her sandals and cotton dress, and dived into the pool.

The water was surprisingly warm. She'd expected it to be cold before the sun had a chance to warm it more. But this was Greece, not England, and things were much warmer here.

She swam around for a while until her fingers began to prune, and then she got out, walked back to the lounger, and dried her hair with her towel.

Once it was dry enough not to drip, she spread the towel out on the chair and laid out on it, letting the sun warm her face and body.

She closed her eyes and lay still as she let the sounds, the smell, and the warmth of the sun gently lull her into a peaceful doze. It felt so relaxing to just lay there calmly and restfully while the chaos of excited holiday makers screamed around her, adding to her relaxed feeling.

She wasn't sure how long she'd laid there but it seemed like at least half an hour or more when she thought she should turn over to get her back into the sun for a while, and get her bottle of orange juice out of her tote bag and have a drink.

She turned over before opening her eyes because she didn't want to squint in the glare of the sun.

Even though she was moving her body she was still wrapped in her own peaceful reverie until Ted's sudden voice brought her out of it. "I thought you were asleep."

She turned towards his voice and saw that he was laying on a towel on the lounge chair beside her. He was laying on his stomach, propped up on his elbows with a book in front of him. His hair was messy as though it had gotten wet while swimming and dried in the sun.

She had no idea that he was there at all. "How long have you been there?"

He grinned and his face lit up with the smile as it usually did. Sofia realised she loved it when that happened.

He said, "I'd just got out of the pool when I saw you arrive and jump in. I thought I'd come over to see you once you were laid down, but by the time I picked up my stuff and walked over, you looked like you were fast asleep so I didn't want to disturb you. But now that you're awake..." He leaned over and kissed her without finishing his sentence. Sofia instinctively leaned in to kiss him too.

She was both surprised and pleased by both his kiss and her response. It felt so natural.

As their lips parted, Ted said, "I missed you this morning. It would have been nice waking up together."

The way he spoke and acted, it seemed to her as though he was automatically assuming that they were a couple now. And although it was what she wanted more than anything, there was still a couple of things in the way. So she decided to bring them up and see what he said, rather than assume what he was thinking.

"I wasn't sure if it was a good idea to wake up with you."

Ted looked genuinely confused. "Why not?"

"Because I have a boyfriend." Sofia braced herself for a negative reaction. She really didn't want to hurt Ted, but she was already in a relationship with another man. But Ted's reaction surprised her.

He smiled widely and laughed. "No you don't."

Sofia was the one that was confused now. "Yes I do. I told you that when we first met."

Ted laughed again. "Yeah, I know what you told me, but I didn't believe it then, and I certainly don't believe it after last night."

Sofia didn't know what to say. She sat up, took out her bottle of juice and had a drink from it. As she put it back in her bag, Ted sat up facing her, took both her hands in his and said, "You told me that you were seeing someone. But you're holidaying alone, so it can't be much of a relationship can it?

"You also told me that the reason he isn't with you is because you needed a break from him, so much so that you've come to another country to get away from him. And then after last night...well...I figured he can't mean that much to you, plus I think you and me have a better relationship than you and him. Don't you?"

Sofia wanted to deny it but she couldn't. And also, she was secretly thrilled that Ted considered them to be in a relationship. She felt almost giddy with excitement.

But calmly, she said, "And what about your other relationship with your wife? You only just got divorced before you came here. Literally the day before, wasn't it? So how do you feel about her now that you're newly divorced?"

Ted laughed again and moved from sitting on his lounger to hers. As he sat next to her, he affectionately put his hand on her thigh and said, "Yes I did only recently get divorced, but we split up months ago. In fact, the marriage was over long before we split up and we should have divorced sooner, but we were both too idle to do it.

"I swear to you that I'm not harbouring any loving feelings towards my ex-wife. In fact, it feels good to officially be able to use the 'ex' part when I refer to her. So now you tell me. Are you harbouring any loving feelings to what I assume is now your ex too?"

Sofia liked his logical way of looking at it. "You make it all sound so simple."

"It is simple," he told her honestly. "You either love someone or you don't. There is no middle ground. If you have to think about whether you want to be with them or not, then clearly you don't love them. You WANT to. But you don't."

She couldn't argue with his logic, and she didn't want to either. Ted wanted to be with her and she wanted to be with him too. And right now that was all that mattered. "I'm not harbouring anything except a desire to jump in the pool again and cool off."

Ted stood up and grabbed her hand. "Then let's do it."

He ran towards the pool, dragging a screaming and laughing Sofia with him and they both jumped in.

After a swim, a playful game of chasing each other and then a loving embrace in the water they went and laid back on their chairs in the sun to dry off and relax for a while.

When they'd had enough of being at the pool, they packed up their belongings and strolled to the onsite cafe for a late lunch.

Back at their rooms they parted. Ted went to his room for a nap while Sofia made herself a cup of coffee and sat out on her patio, feeling relaxed and happy.

Then seemingly as though from nowhere, Amy appeared with a cup of hot steaming beverage of her own. She came straight up to Sofia and sat down beside her. "Hey Sofia. How's it going with you and your new beau?"

Sofia laughed at the old fashioned term coming from such a young woman. "Couldn't be better, actually."

Amy looked intrigued. "Oh, do tell."

Sofia told her about her final encounter with Mario when he wouldn't take no for an answer and how seeing them together had upset Ted but it had all worked out in the end and about the wonderful evening she'd spent with Ted and their time at the pool.

Amy seemed genuinely pleased for her. "Oh, you're so lucky. I bet you never imagined that you'd find your soulmate here on this little island. Too bad you have to face going home and finishing it with your ex."

Sofia thought how funny it was that both Amy and Ted automatically referred to Jason as her ex. But then again, it felt like he already was, at least in Sofia's mind. "What about you, Amy. How are things turning out for you?"

Amy laughed. "You mean between me and my ex?"

"You're kidding! Have you two broken up?"

Amy put on a sad, yet thoughtful smile. "No. Not yet. I think it would be terrible to split up when we only have a couple of days left here. I'm just waiting until we get home and then I'll leave him quietly."

Sofia felt bad for her new friend. "So there really is no hope?"

"None. He's just so selfish, but I didn't realise it until we came here and I had nothing else to do but notice how selfish and narcissistic he is. Usually I'm too distracted with work and other things. But here there's no distractions. Just me and him, so my attention has been completely on him. Plus I've had plenty of time to think."

Sofia wasn't sure what to say. "Looks like this holiday will be life-altering for both of us in different ways."

Amy looked wistfully out over the gardens. "Yeah, but it will still have a happy outcome for us both."

Sofia liked Amy and wished that there was something she could do to help her. But there wasn't. She also wasn't sure that her own situation would end well for her either.

She knew that no matter what, she was going to end her relationship with Jason.

But what if Ted didn't want to see her anymore once they returned home? What if he only saw their relationship as a holiday romance?

And it was easy to have a good time here because, as Amy said, there are no distractions and plenty of time. So even if they did continue to see each other, would the huge distance between where they lived be a problem or would the usual life and work distractions get in their way?

She had no idea. At the moment she was enjoying a holiday romance and even if she never saw Ted again, she knew she'd always treasure the time they had together.

She'd temporarily forgotten about the other people in their lives while she was here, and had no idea how negatively it was about to affect them.

Chapter 12

Friday. Day 8

Sofia woke up with a feeling that she could only describe as tranquil.

The previous evening, she and Ted had gone out for dinner at one of the local bars and then went back to his room and, after a couple of drinks, had gone to bed and drifted to sleep in each other's arms.

And Friday began in the same, peaceful, relaxing way, but little did she know, that it certainly wasn't going to end that way.

Sofia had spent the morning sitting on her couch at the bottom of her bed, watching TV and doing some knitting that she'd brought with her.

Then in the afternoon, she and Ted had sat in a local bar where it was cool compared to the heat outside, and had a couple of cold beers and a few snacks.

That evening, they had dinner together on Sofia's patio. She'd chilled some wine and made them a bean and chickpea salad and a pan of pasta and vegetables in a tomato sauce and had fried some bread in garlic butter. She thought it was a pretty substantial meal, considering she had no oven to bake things in.

After they'd eaten, they washed and dried the dirty dishes and went back out onto the patio to finish their bottle of wine.

They chatted happily about their lives and their work and it seemed they had a lot in common.

Ted was a computer programmer and worked for one of the biggest banks in the UK, and although he had an office at their head office in London, he mostly worked from home.

Sofia told him that she too worked from home working on her hand-made wedding gowns. Ted seemed impressed and even interested to see some of her work. So when they went back to their rooms, she showed him the bodice of the dress she was currently beading. Ted was extremely complimentary about her talent, and she loved how different his attitude was to Jason's. Ted was also full of admiration about her ability to turn her hobby into a profitable business.

Sofia was equally impressed with how Ted was so good at his job that his company were happy to let him work most days at home rather than lose him. And that they also contracted him out to other companies because, apparently, there was no one as adept at computer programming as Ted, even though he didn't seem to think that his natural programming talent was such a big deal.

Sofia now felt so relaxed and happy sitting there in the evening, drinking wine with Ted and learning all about him.

Ted smiled at her and said, "You know, I don't think I know any women who are as savvy as you. You not only own your own home outright, but you know how to run your own business, and your dressmaking skills have to be the best I've ever seen. You really are a smart and talented person.

Sofia just loved sitting back and absorbing his praise. "You're not so bad yourself. You live in the very swanky London suburb of Holland Park. Most people can only dream of being able to afford to live there.

"And you're so good at your job that the bank lets you stay at home and work, even though they much prefer to have you in your office every day."

"Well, to be honest, I get more work done at home than I do when I'm in my office because people there never stop interrupting me."

Sofia liked his humbleness. He genuinely didn't see anything worth bragging about regarding his work or where he lived.

Then suddenly, their peace was loudly interrupted by the arrival of an extremely drunken Caroline.

"So there you are, you rotten bastard. You've been avoiding me the last few days. Why haven't you come to see me? I've been waiting."

Caroline stood on the lawn in front of the patio swaying slightly as she spoke. Sofia had forgotten Caroline even existed until that moment, but obviously she thought that she still had something going with Ted.

Ted didn't move. He simply stared at Caroline with an unreadable expression on his face. "I haven't been avoiding you. I simply haven't seen you."

Caroline screamed at him, "Don't lie to me! I've been looking everywhere for you." She swung out her left arm as she said it as if to indicate exactly where 'everywhere' was. "But you haven't been anywhere. So I stayed in my room all day in case you called round. But you didn't even walk past. And my room's only over there." Again she swung her arm out as she said it to demonstrate where 'there' was. But to swing her arm in the direction of her room, she had to turn around, but that caused her to stagger and nearly lose her balance.

Ted gave her a half smile. "And you were drinking the whole time while you were waiting?"

Sofia had to suppress a small laugh at Ted's humour, but Caroline was too drunk to notice the sarcasm. "No I wasn't. I've been out tonight looking for you everywhere."

Ted smiled even more. "And drinking everywhere too, I see."

His flippant remark only enraged the already frustrated Caroline. She began to cry as she shouted, "It's not funny! We had something special. I knew you really liked me. Why are you with her now?" Caroline's swinging arm now loosely swung up in Sofia's direction before flopping back heavily to her side.

Ted spoke quietly so that only Sofia could hear him. "I think I need to tie up this loose end." And with that, he stepped down off the patio, put his arm across the shoulders of the sobbing Caroline and walked her away.

Sofia sat feeling stunned for a few seconds. How quickly their quiet evening had changed. And now Ted was gone and she wasn't sure when he'd be back.

She drank the last sip of wine from her glass and took it back to the kitchen for a refill. She took Ted's drink inside too and left it in the fridge.

Sitting back down outside, she heard a familiar voice from the darkness call her name. "Sofia!"

Looking up she saw Mario striding towards her across the garden. He looked pleased to see her and stopped just in front of her patio. "How are you?"

"Fine," she responded, feeling cautious about why he was there. Maybe he was another loose end that needed tying up.

Mario was still smiling. "Why don't we have a drink together? I can go and get another bottle of wine."

Sofia was bowled over by his sudden eagerness to be with her, especially after their last heated encounter. It was obvious that he was lonely and thought that Sofia was too. She wanted to get rid of him fast. Even if she wasn't with Ted, she still wanted nothing to do with Mario.

She decided that the best approach was a straight forward one, so that he'd be in no doubt once and for all that she wanted nothing to do with him. "No."

"Why not?" He looked genuinely confused, but she didn't like his assumption that she had to give him a reason for not wanting to be with him.

"I don't want to. Just because I'm sitting here on my own having a quiet drink doesn't mean I'm looking for company."

She saw his expression instantly change from confused to angry.

He took a deep breath and held his palms up in a completely confused gesture, but his voice was filled with anger. "What is wrong with you? I come and ask you if you'd like to have a drink with me. That is all. Yet I get such a hostile tone from you."

Sofia snapped back at him straight away before he could say any more. "DON'T try and put this back on me. I said no to you the other day and I'm saying no to you again. This is MY room. You came here to me both times. I've NEVER come to your room looking for you so DON'T try and make me the villain. Now go away and don't say another word or I'm going to start screaming as loud as I can to attract the security guards. GO!" She pointed to her right in the direction of the path that would lead him away from her room.

Mario looked stunned while she admonished him, but the look on his face also told her that he believed every word that she said about screaming. And she did.

He turned and walked briskly away, hunching his shoulders and having an angry-sounding conversation with himself in Italian as he went.

Sofia sat back in her chair, relieved that her threat had worked. She hadn't wanted to create a scene but was prepared to if Mario hadn't taken no for an answer. Guys like him could quickly become a real problem if you weren't firm with them right from the start.

But she was still wondering what was happening with Ted and Caroline.

Then she noticed an argument going on in Lenore and Mick's room. Their patio door was closed and they had the TV or radio on, so Sofia couldn't hear what they were saying, but the tone wasn't good.

Mostly it sounded like Lenore was doing all the yelling with Mick interjecting now and then, but not getting a chance to say much.

The evening was not what Sofia had been expecting. She'd envisioned a romantic night with just her and Ted having a quiet meal and a couple of glasses of wine. She hadn't counted on the angry interruptions that had happened and were still happening.

Suddenly, she heard a patio door open and close and briefly heard Lenore screaming, "Don't you dare walk out on me. I'm talking to you. Don't you DARE..." The rest of her words were muffled by the slamming door.

Then she saw Mick jump off their patio onto the grass. He exhaled deeply and looked around as though he didn't know what to do next.

He noticed Sofia and nodded at her. "I suppose you heard all that."

Sofia felt uncomfortable. "Not really, but it sounded very heated."

Mick stepped up onto her patio and sat in Ted's empty chair. He looked more sad than angry. "I really don't know what to do any more. I thought retirement would make it better between us but it seems to be worse. Lenore is just so angry with me all the time and I have no idea why."

Sofia didn't know how to respond so she said nothing.

Mick was rubbing both his palms together while staring out across the gardens. Then he turned to Sofia and said, "Do you have a woman's perspective on this that might help me?"

Sofia didn't want to get involved in another couple's arguments. "I really don't know what to say because I don't know either of you well enough to know what's going on and it's none of my business anyway."

Mick looked at her pleadingly. "Please, Sofia. Just tell me anything that might help. Honestly it's impossible to make this situation any worse because I've just had enough. I can't take it anymore."

Sofia felt sad for him because he looked totally dejected and helpless.

She paused for a few moments before speaking. "Well, there's a saying that people will treat you as badly as you allow them to. And no woman will respect a man who allows her to treat him badly. In fact, women hate being able to treat someone like that. It frustrates them that they're allowed to be so nasty and so it only exacerbates the situation and makes them turn on you even more."

Mick stared at her as she spoke and the tightness in his face began to loosen. It was as though he completely recognised himself and his wife in Sofia's words.

He continued to look at her for a few more seconds after she finished speaking, then turned to stare out across the gardens. "I feel like I came and sat at the feet of the Buddha. Those were wise words indeed."

He turned back to look at Sofia again. "You're absolutely spot on, but the question is, what am I going to do about it?"

Sofia said nothing and Mick looked down at the table, as though thinking hard.

Then without another word, he stood up, stepped off the patio and wandered off into the darkness.

Sofia watched him go and wondered if she'd said the wrong thing. She hadn't meant to imply that it was Mick's fault, but rather it was something that they both needed to change.

Just as Mick disappeared from sight, she heard a patio door opening again and then Lenore appeared, standing on the grass looking around and then came up onto Sofia's patio as soon as she noticed she was there.

"Where's Mick?" She demanded. It was said so directly that Sofia instantly felt like she was being blamed for the fact that Lenore couldn't see her husband.

"I don't know."

"You saw him, didn't you? Where'd he go?"

Sofia didn't like this hostile side of Lenore. "Yes, I saw him. We spoke briefly and then he walked away but he never said where he was going."

Lenore became even angrier at this news. "So what the hell did you say to him to make him leave?"

Sofia had had enough. Lenore had no business being angry with her after the huge row she'd heard her having with Mick.

She tried to hold her temper as she spoke. "I hardly think it was anything I said to him. It was you that drove him away with all your screaming and yelling."

"That's none of your business," Lenore snapped.

Sofia let out a slight laugh at Lenore's irony. "Oh yes it is if you come stamping out here accusing me of upsetting your husband when it was YOU he was wanting to get away from. Fight your own battles with him and leave me out of it. Go!" She pointed towards Lenore's room as she said the last word.

Lenore looked as though she was going to say something else and then thought better of it and left, disappearing around the joining wall.

Sofia was relieved that she was gone but wondered how the encounter would impact on their friendship the next time they saw each other.

Then she thought about Ted again and wondered where he was.

At that precise moment he appeared in the distance, walking across the garden towards her. She went inside and retrieved his glass of wine from the fridge.

He greeted her with a kiss and sat down. Sofia asked him, "So what happened?"

Ted pulled a funny face and smiled. "Well, it was unpleasant. Caroline was really drunk and really argumentative and wouldn't accept that I didn't want to see her again."

He laughed at himself. "Stupidly, I tried to reason with her but it was no use and she was crying so much. In the end there was nothing else to do but walk away and not look back. And she hurled abuse at me the whole time calling me a coward for leaving and a horrible person for making her think I cared about her. But I never cared about her so why would I have wanted her to think that I did?" He laughed again.

"Do you think she'll continue to harass you?"

Ted smiled. "Oh I doubt it. When she wakes up tomorrow and remembers parts of tonight, she'll probably be too embarrassed by her drunken behaviour."

"I hope you're right."

"Oh I am," he said, still laughing. "She was definitely embarrassing herself tonight, but too drunk to know it yet."

"She's not the only one who's been a problem tonight."

Ted looked surprised. "Really? Who else has been behaving badly?"

Sofia told him about Mario and Mick and Lenore. Ted listened to it all with great interest and then laughed again. "Good grief! How long was I gone?"

Sofia laughed too. "I know, right? It was unbelievable. Just one thing happened after another, and Lenore had only just gone inside and shut the door when I saw you coming back, so it really has been non-stop."

Ted laughed too. "Looks like everyone's angry with us tonight."

Sofia certainly agreed with that. Not only was everyone angry with her here, but she also knew that once she got home and ended her relationship with Jason, he'd be angry with her too. How could she have ever known that her quiet little holiday to this small island would become so full of negative emotions.

Ted put his arm around her. "I know what we need to do. Drink more wine." He picked up his glass and took a sip. Sofia did the same.

They sat and talked quietly for some time while they drank a couple more glasses of wine.

After a while Mick returned. He stopped in front of Sofia's patio swaying slightly from one or two drinks too many. "Sofia, I'm glad we spoke earlier because you were completely right. I do let Lenore treat me badly, and do you know why? Because I always thought it best to say nothing when she was angry."

He put his hands in his pockets and looked briefly at the ground before continuing. "But you know what? It didn't work. It didn't ever make her less angry. And like you said all I was doing was allowing her to go on treating me badly because I never told her to stop."

"But no more. Either she stops or I'm leaving, because I don't want things to stay like this, and they will if I let them. So I'm not going to let them." And with that he turned and headed toward his own room.

They heard the patio door open and close and could hear Mick's voice, muffled behind the thick glass, "Lenore, I've been having a good think about us and I've come to a decision. So this is it. I'm not happy with the way things are and I don't think you are either. So this is what's going to happen."

The rest of his words became inaudible as he walked away from the door. Then they heard Lenore's raised voice but she sounded as though she was trying to talk over the top of him rather than shouting.

Ted turned to Sofia and said, "This would be a good time to disappear to my place, shut the door, put some quiet music on to drown out those two, and escape from all this craziness tonight."

Sofia thought it was an excellent suggestion and said, "I'll get my keys and lock my door."

Once inside Ted's room he locked the patio door and drew the curtains behind them.

There was only dim light from a bedside lamp and he put on some romantic-sounding music that Sofia didn't recognise.

Then he put his arms around her and kissed her passionately. She responded eagerly, feeling that there was nowhere on the planet that she wanted to be right now except right here in Ted's arms.

She felt his hand slide down the side of her body as he began to caress her neck with his lips.

She tilted her head back and surrendered willingly into his desire for her.

Chapter 13

Saturday. Day 9

Sofia came awake slowly, listening to the sounds of the Corfu birds. They sounded so different to the birds she was used to hearing back home in Bath in the UK.

She suddenly realised she was naked and then remembered that she was in Ted's room. She opened her eyes and turned over to look at him.

Her movement must have woken him because at that same moment, he opened his eyes, rubbed them and turned to look at Sofia.

Without saying a word, he smiled at her and put his arms around her, drawing her close.

She snuggled up against him.

As she lay there, she wondered what had happened with Lenore and Mick after their heated ultimatum with Mick's insistence that their relationship improve or end.

Laying there naked with Ted, on a warm, quiet morning with only the birds to listen to, Sofia soon found herself drifting back to sleep.

Sometime later she awoke again. "What time is it?"

Ted looked at the alarm clock on his nightstand. "Nine."

Sofia was surprised at how late it was. "Are you kidding? I can't remember the last time I ever slept in this late."

"Well, it was a late night," Ted reminded her. "Especially with all that we got up to once we came inside." He gave her an affectionate squeeze as he said it.

"I wonder if the neighbours kissed and made up last night?"

Ted smiled. "I doubt it. I could still hear them going at it when I was trying to get to sleep."

"It's quiet there now."

"Maybe he left."

Sofia hadn't considered that. She thought they would have sorted out their problems because they'd been together so long.

Ted interrupted her thoughts. "Who cares anyway? They're adults and can sort out their own lives. Fancy going out for breakfast?"

Sofia did. She was hungry. Reluctantly, she broke their embrace and sat up, taking the sheet with her to cover her breasts while she reached for her blouse which was strewn across the floor next to the bed.

Then she put her shorts on, picked up her underwear and keys and headed for the door. "I'll go and get showered. See you soon."

Ted blew her a kiss. She blew one back and left, closing the door behind her.

Despite the tension with all the others the night before, Sofia felt really happy. It felt as though she and Ted were now officially a couple.

She let herself into her dark room and threw open the curtains and the patio door to let in light and fresh air.

This new day felt really good to her and she couldn't remember the last time she felt this happy and content.

She felt fresh and clean after having a shower and Ted arrived at her room soon afterwards and they headed out for breakfast.

They ate in a nearby restaurant and stayed there quite a while and enjoyed two extra cups of coffee as they sat and chatted.

As they were leaving, Ted asked, "So what do you want to do today? Do you fancy the beach?"

Sofia was pleasantly surprised at his natural assumption that they were going to spend all day together. "Yeah, a swim and a quiet read would be nice."

They stopped at the little supermarket to get a couple of drinks to take with them. Ted also picked up a large packet of potato chips. "Lunch," he said, holding them up for her to see. She smiled at his boyish expression that she'd come to love.

Ted was such a laid-back and easy-going person and while she liked that about him, she still hadn't quite gotten used to it.

He was the opposite of Jason who now seemed to her like a really insecure male. Being with Ted was making her see Jason in a whole new light, and it wasn't flattering at all.

Ted seemed to want to be with her. It was that plain and simple. And easy.

Jason, on the other hand, seemed to always have a hidden agenda. He always wanted to know what she'd been doing since he last saw her and whatever she told him, he belittled it.

One day recently, she told him she'd been to the supermarket to get some groceries, and he made an insulting remark about women always wanting to shop. And when she said she'd run into an old friend and had coffee with them, he responded with, "I bet there was a ton of girlie gossip to catch up on."

It was as though he wasn't just trying to belittle her, but trying to sound as though he was a "big man" while she was "just a little woman." It was an attitude that up until now, she had disliked, but tolerated.

But after spending time with someone as unpretentious as Ted, she now hated Jason's attitude and definitely didn't want to put up with it any more.

It was like she'd told Mick the previous evening; people will treat you as badly as you allow them to. But she wouldn't any longer. She would continue to keep her phone switched off while she was here so that she wouldn't have to speak to Jason, and she'd end the relationship as soon as she returned home.

Even if things didn't work out between her and Ted, she'd rather be alone than suffer Jason's constant put-downs any more.

But right now she was with Ted and loving every minute of it. So she would focus only on being here with him and let the future take care of itself.

She was more than halfway through her holiday now so she wanted to make the most of the few days they had left.

She went back to her room to change into her bikini and wore a long, cotton shirt over the top of it.

Ted went to his room to get changed too, and then they walked through the resort, through the pool area, and out onto the beach.

It was a beautiful, warm day with not a cloud in the sky. The water lapped gently at the white sand and Sofia and Ted walked barefoot through it as they looked for a place to sit.

There wasn't many people there and soon they saw the familiar sight of Lenore and Mick.

Ted had already chosen a spot to lay out their towels before they saw the other couple, but Mick and Lenore were far enough away and looked like they were deep in a heated discussion.

As they slipped off their clothes and headed down to the water, Ted asked, "Do you think they've been at it all night?"

Sofia said, "It wouldn't surprise me," and then turned her complete attention back to herself and Ted.

After a leisurely swim they went back and laid on their towels, got out a book each, and started reading.

It felt so great to be there with Ted on this quiet beach on a warm and sunny day. And just like the night before, she felt there was nowhere else on earth she'd rather be right now.

Suddenly, Ted broke her reverie. "Here comes trouble at 3 o'clock."

Sofia looked to her left and saw Lenore and Mick walking their way. But they were still deep in conversation so failed to notice Sofia and Ted.

Sofia watched them leave the beach and head back through the pool area, talking the whole time. "I can't read the mood between them at all."

Ted smiled. "Me neither. No doubt we'll know soon enough."

"I just hope they don't blame me if they break up. Lenore was pretty mad at me last night."

"So what if she is? We don't have to put up with them much longer anyway."

Sofia went back to her book. She didn't want to be reminded that their holiday would end soon.

They stayed at the beach for most of the day and alternated between swimming, reading, talking and eating potato chips. It was the most relaxed and happy day that Sofia had ever known.

Later in the afternoon, they made their way back to their rooms.

They showered and changed and sat outside on Sofia's patio and sipped a couple of glasses of wine.

While they were there, Lenore and Mick's room remained closed but Sofia knew they were in there because she heard them moving around.

She discussed it with Ted. He said he'd heard them too, but like Sofia, he had no idea if it was a make up or break up situation.

They took a stroll out to the supermarket as the sun went down and bought something for dinner plus they each bought a few other supplies.

Sofia put her own groceries away in her kitchen and then locked up and joined Ted in his room where they planned to have dinner alone, or as Ted put it, "A Caroline-Mario-Lenore-and-Mick-free meal."

They agreed that if they stayed inside behind a locked door, no one could interrupt them again. They also decided to keep quiet and not put any music on either so that not even Lenore and Mick would know they were there.

They cooked the food together in the small, limited kitchen and ate sitting on the couch and washed the food down with a couple of beers.

Afterwards, they turned off the lights, undressed each other, and had sex that Sofia found loving as well as intimate. Then they lay in each other's arms and drifted peacefully to sleep.

It was a perfect end to a perfect day.

Chapter 14

Sunday. Day 10

Sofia woke up and saw the sun shining in around the edges of the heavy patio curtains.

She looked over at Ted laying peacefully beside her.

She squeezed his arm and said, "I'm going for a shower," then slipped quickly out of bed, put on her clothes and headed out to her own room.

The sun dazzled her as she moved the curtain to one side and slid the door open, before stepping out into the warm day and closing the door behind her.

There were already plenty of people milling around but no one seemed to notice her as she stepped down off Ted's patio, crossed the lawn in front of Lenore and Mick's room and stepped up onto her own patio. She did notice that there was no sign of life yet at Lenore and Mick's place.

Her own closed-up room was dark and cool. She let it stay that way while she showered.

Once dressed, she pulled back her own heavy curtains, opened the big sliding, glass door and let the light and warmth wash into her room.

She went to the kitchen and put the kettle on to boil while she sat outside and towelled her wet hair.

The day was already warm even though it was still only a little after 8 a.m.

Soon she heard the kettle boil so she went back inside, hung her towel back in the bathroom and made herself a cup of hot, black coffee that she took outside with her and sat at her small table.

Within minutes, Ted arrived and he too was freshly showered and carrying a cup of coffee. He sat down in the empty chair and leaned over to kiss her.

She returned his kiss and loved their easy relationship and the fact that they had nothing else to do except be together.

As they broke their kiss Ted looked up at the clear blue sky. "Another beautiful day, I see."

Sofia looked up too. "In every way."

Ted put his hand on Sofia's thigh under the table. She was wearing shorts so his hand touched her flesh. He smiled his now-so-familiar smile at her. "I never knew I'd enjoy Corfu this much."

She returned his smile. "I never thought I'd meet someone like you."

Ted leaned over and kissed her again. "But I'm glad you did."

As they sipped their coffee they discussed their plans for the day, starting with breakfast, which they planned to eat out.

So once they finished their coffee, Ted returned his cup to his own kitchen and locked up his room while Sofia did the same, and then they strolled hand in hand to a local restaurant for breakfast.

Sofia just loved everything about being here. The great weather, the laid back atmosphere of the restaurants and bars, the pool area, the beach and the way everything was within walking distance.

But mostly she loved being here with Ted and what an easy relationship they had here. Every day, all they had to do was decide which fun things they were going to do.

It was unbelievable that it was all going to end soon.

They sat on the verandah of the restaurant and ate a filling breakfast of potatoes, tomatoes, mushrooms, baked beans and toasted muffins, all washed down with a glass of orange juice and two more cups of coffee.

The waiter took their plates away while they sipped their second cup.

Ted said, "This would be a good day to relax by the pool."

Sofia agreed and added, "It's Sunday today so it might be crowded."

Ted smiled. "It doesn't matter what day of the week it is to all the tourists here."

Sofia realised how silly it was to worry about it being the weekend. "Oh, yeah."

Ted's smile disappeared. "It's also our last Sunday here."

Sofia looked wistfully out at the street and all the people passing by. "Don't remind me. I hate to think about leaving. I feel like I live here now."

Ted laughed. "Me too. I find it hard to remember that I have another life that I have to get back to soon."

"Then don't think about it," Sofia cut in quickly. "Let's just enjoy this life in Greece while we can."

"I'll drink to that," said Ted, raising his coffee cup.

Sofia raised hers too and they chinked their cups together as she said, "Cheers."

They both took a sip of hot coffee and Ted said, "How about that day at the pool then?"

"Yeah, let's do it."

When they finished their coffee, Ted paid the bill and they walked back to their rooms.

As they arrived they were surprised to hear Lenore laughing. They found her and Mick sitting out on their patio and judging by all the crockery on the table, it was clear that they'd just finished breakfast.

The most surprising thing was that they seemed to be really happy together. Almost acting like a newly married couple the way they were smiling, sitting close together and holding hands.

Mick smiled at Ted and Sofia when he saw them standing on the lawn. "Hey, come up and join us. Want coffee?"

He half got up out of his chair as he spoke, but Ted put his hand up to signal him not to bother. "No thanks. We've just come back from having breakfast and several cups of coffee, so we're fine. We were just going to get ready and head off to the pool."

Lenore smiled at Mick. "Why don't we go too?"

Mick turned to Ted. "Mind if we come with you?"

"The more the merrier."

"Great. We'll deal with these dirty dishes and get ready."

Lenore and Mick stood up and started clearing the table. Ted briefly kissed Sofia, said, "See you soon," and headed off to his own room.

Sofia felt momentarily annoyed. She had been looking forward to spending time alone with Ted and didn't want to have another couple with them.

But her feeling of annoyance was over in a second because she was also intrigued to find out what had happened between Lenore and Mick. She'd felt certain that their marriage was rocky at best, especially after their last few days of solitude and deep conversations.

Sofia had thought they were discussing how to divide up their assets and what they were going to say to the rest of the family.

Yet here they were, acting completely the opposite. It seemed as though they'd never been happier.

Sofia went back to her own room lost in her thoughts and feeling intrigued. She would have to find some time alone today with Lenore to find out what happened. But she had no idea how she was going to find time to speak to Lenore on her own if the four of them were going to be together.

But she needn't have wondered because as soon as they laid out their towels by the pool, Ted and Mick went for a swim together after Lenore said, "You two go ahead and jump in. Sofia and I need to catch up."

The men couldn't have left them alone faster if they'd tried.

As soon as the men hit the water, Lenore turned to Sofia and said, "I had no idea what you'd said to Mick the other night and I thought it was going to hurt our relationship. But instead it had the biggest impact and for all the right reasons."

"What did I say exactly?" Sofia had only spoken briefly to Mick and wasn't sure what she'd said that could have been so positively impactful.

"He said you'd told him that people will treat you as badly as you allow them to. So he wasn't mad at me for anything I'd said, which is what I thought at first.

"No. He was annoyed with himself for being such a wimp all these years. So he said it wasn't going to go on any longer so either things would change or he would leave, because we were both making ourselves miserable."

Lenore took a brief pause to look round and make sure the men were still in the water and then she continued. "And you were right about me too. I WAS treating him badly, but only because he was allowing me to. So we were both at fault.

"Luckily, we were both adult enough to admit our faults and not blame the other. It was hard for me to respect a man who was so weak that he'd let me put him down all the time. And it was hard for him to love a woman who demeaned him all the time.

"So we both agreed to change, especially Mick who was determined to put a stop to how things were.

"Honestly Sofia, I've never seen him like this, ever. He really put his foot down and told me exactly how things were going to be from now on and said that my behaviour and attitude towards him was both childish and humiliating. And I think it was the word childish that struck a chord with me the most because he was right. I had been behaving childish. Probably more brattish.

"I was so ashamed at all the humiliation I'd been putting him through, and he reminded me of hundreds of instances when I'd said terrible things to him.

"We talked it out for hours and hours. We haven't even slept much lately. But it didn't matter because we had so much to talk about and so many decisions about the changes we're going to make.

"But honestly Sofia, seeing Mick stand up for himself this way has given me a whole new respect for him. Why did I ever treat him so badly? And why did he never once tell me to stop?

"But it's different now. And so fast! Once we started respecting each other, everything just seemed to change for the better. I don't think we've ever been this happy before."

Lenore took Sofia by the hand which took her by surprise. She squeezed Sofia's hand between her own two palms."I think...no, I believe, that you were sent to Corfu to save my marriage, because we knew we couldn't go on the way we were much longer. I think we both knew that, and that's why we started travelling. It was an attempted distraction. We both weren't happy and were trying to fool ourselves into thinking that being somewhere else would solve our relationship issues. And in a way it did, thanks to you."

Sofia didn't know what to say. She hoped that Lenore was wrong and that Sofia's reason for being in Corfu wasn't to save someone's marriage. She wanted it to be to meet Ted.

To Lenore she said, "I didn't save your marriage. You and Mick did. Goodness knows how much talking and reconciling you've both done lately but that had nothing to do with me."

Lenore released Sofia's hand and said, "It's like our recent talking was a fire that raged for a while and now has finished and a phoenix has risen from the ashes. But you were the spark that ignited the fire, and there can't be any fire without a spark."

Sofia smiled. "OK. I give up. And you're welcome."

Both women laughed and simultaneously looked out at the men to see if they were still in the water. Ted and Mick were hanging onto the edge of the pool and talking.

Lenore turned to Sofia. "Now it's your turn. What's going on with you and Teddy Bear? You seemed close this morning. Almost like a real couple."

"It feels like we are a real couple." Sofia continued to update Lenore on the situation with Caroline and how she and Ted were now spending all their time together.

Lenore seemed pleased with this news, but asked, "Don't you have a boyfriend at home waiting in the wings?"

Sofia looked over at Ted as she spoke. "Yeah, but like you, I wasn't happy with my relationship, only mine is like the Titanic and is sinking fast. And unlike your relationship, it can't be saved because there's only one of us that's behaving badly and it's not me.

"What's worse is that his bad behaviour has devolved over the years and now he's just so rude to me most of the time. I think it's mostly because he's jealous that I work from home while he has to go out to work every day. It seems to drive him crazy that I sit and sew every day.

"But if he really cared about me then he'd want me to enjoy what I do instead of belittling me all the time."

Lenore agreed with her. "Well I thought that it couldn't be a good relationship if you had to leave the country to get away from him."

Sofia looked at Lenore and they both laughed. "Yeah, it is a bit of a giveaway. No matter what happens between me and Ted though, I can never be with Jason again."

"Will you see Ted once you get home?"

"I hope so, but he hasn't mentioned anything yet. And I'm not going to push it because even if I never see him again I'll always be grateful for our time together here in Corfu. This is a holiday I'll definitely remember."

"You two also live quite a distance apart, don't you?"

Sofia sighed. "Yeah that's another hurdle if we come to it. Seeing each other would be do-able though because Ted works from home too so neither of us has a 9 to 5 job to get in the way."

"I'm eager to find out how this ends for you. I hope he does want to see you again."

"I want to see him now while I still can. Come on. Let's join the guys." She stood up, stripped off her shorts and top and walked towards the pool. Lenore joined her and they both jumped in together.

Chapter 15

Monday. Day 11

The next morning, after a leisurely, late breakfast on Sofia's patio, she and Ted headed off for a walk into the nearby town of Kavos.

It was well-known for its many bars and night clubs that stayed open well into the early hours of the morning. Sofia was glad they were staying outside the town but within easy walking distance.

The road leading into Kavos was narrow with no footpaths but it was an interesting walk as they passed fields of olive trees and many local houses which were so different from British homes and they were both amazed at all the different fruits growing in the gardens, including grapes, bananas and oranges.

It only took 20 minutes to reach Kavos which was a busy town, full of souvenir shops, bars and restaurants.

They weaved their way through the busy, crowded streets, looking in a few shops along the way.

Eventually Sofia said she was too hot to walk anymore, so they searched for a somewhat quiet bar bought two glasses of cold orange juice, and sat out on the breezy back veranda to drink it.

While they were there a waiter brought them a menu which listed only fast food such as burgers, chips and salad.

Ted ordered some salad and chips and they ate it with a cold glass of beer each. The Greek beer was so much lighter and more refreshing than British beer.

They took their time, and when they were finished they made their way back through the town and this time they walked back along the beach, walking through a couple of rock pools along the way.

Sofia was having a great day and loving every minute of being with Ted, even when she slipped on wet rocks and Ted had to hold her up and they both laughed the whole time.

Usually she didn't enjoy too much company with other people.

She had lots of friends that would drop by her house for a cup of tea or coffee and she was always glad to see them. But within less than an hour she was ready for them to leave so she'd stop talking as much in the hope that they'd take the subtle social cue and go, which they usually did.

Even with Jason she was happy to see him and spend time with him, but not every day. So she was surprised that she was happy to spend every waking and sleeping minute with Ted. She'd even come to notice his lack of presence in the brief, few times she'd been on her own to shower and get ready to see him again.

She wondered if maybe it felt different because they were on holiday and had not much else to do. Or maybe it was her attraction to Ted. She couldn't imagine being at her house back in Bath and not wanting him to be there. She felt like she would always want to be with him.

They soon arrived back at their resort and passed through the pool area and made their way back to their rooms.

They were holding hands the whole way and Ted led Sofia straight to his room, closed the door, switched on the air conditioning, and poured them both a cold glass of cola. Sofia was thirsty and drank it quickly.

Ted sat on the edge the bed and patted the space next to him so Sofia sat with him.

He looked serious as he spoke which made Sofia briefly worried about what he was going to say. But she relaxed as soon as he started to speak.

"Sofia, I know that you live in Bath and I live in London, but it's only a couple of hours drive and I'd like to see you again once we go home."

Sofia was thrilled. These were the words she'd been longing to hear. "I want that too. I can't believe we have to leave here in a few days."

"Me neither. But just because the holiday's ending doesn't mean that we have to. I'm not even sure if we'll feel the same once we get home and our usual lives get in the way, but I'd like to try."

Sofia smiled. "I've been wondering the exact same thing. We have no distractions here or family or friends to get in our way so it will be different once we get home. Plus we live so far apart, so we can't be together all the time like we are here."

Ted smiled too. "Yeah, I know it will be different, but it won't be bad. We'll adjust."

"Damn straight we will." Sofia laughed and Ted laughed too and said, "Then it's official. We'll exchange details before we leave and arrange to meet up soon."

"Damn straight," said Sofia, and they both laughed again.

They finished their drinks quickly. Ted took the glasses into the kitchen.

When he came back he sat next to Sofia again and kissed her.

Their kisses intensified and he put his arms around her, pushing her gently back onto the bed.

They made love in a way that seemed more intimate than ever before. Sofia wasn't sure if it was her imagination or if it was because their relationship had gone to another level now that they were going to carry on seeing each other.

They spent time in foreplay exploring each other's body and taking it in turn to bring each other almost to climax over and over, until sexual excitement overwhelmed them and they gave in to full intercourse.

Afterwards they lay quietly side by side for a while without speaking.

Eventually, Sofia broke the silence. 'You're amazing." She turned on her side to look at him as she spoke.

Ted stretched out his arm and wrapped it around her naked body, pulling her close. "No. We're amazing."

And right then, in that moment, she felt she loved him. Had she loved him before that moment? She wasn't sure. But she was sure that right now she'd fallen in love with him.

Ted turned to her and said, "Now that we've been dirty, how about jumping in the pool and getting clean?"

"Sounds good to me."

They broke their embrace and hunted around on the floor for their clothes. Sofia dressed, kissed Ted and slipped out the door. Back in her room she changed into her bikini, pulled a long, cotton slip-on shirt/dress over the top, put on a pair of flip-flops and put a few things in her tote bag, including a book, a towel and a bottle of water.

Soon Ted arrived and they walked over to the pool, spread their towels out, stripped of their outer clothing and jumped into the water, which felt momentarily cold but welcoming.

They spent time splashing around, embracing, kissing and talking. Ted asked her about Jason and if she'd spoken to him while she was here.

She told him, "To be honest, I've had my phone switched off all the time I've been here because I don't want to talk to anyone, especially him. I came here to get away from him so that we could both have some space and time to think about if we want to stay together. But really, I think I just wanted to end it but I thought at least coming here and saying it was to give me time, at least makes it look like I've given it some thought before I say goodbye to him."

Ted smiled ruefully. "Well, to be honest, as soon as you said you had a boyfriend but you were here alone for 2 weeks without him, I knew the relationship was bad. No way would you holiday without him if you wanted to be with him.”

“It was that obvious, huh?”

“Clear as glass to everyone,” said Ted, pulling her up against him in the water and kissing her again.

When they got out of the pool they laid on their towels to dry off in the sun.

Sofia looked down at her body and could see how tanned she’d gotten while she was here, but it was no wonder considering how much time she’d spent in the sun.

After a while she sat up and got out her watch which was buried under the pile of her neatly folded clothes beside her. “It’s 4 o’clock. Maybe we should head back now. I need to have a shower and wash my hair.”

Ted reluctantly sat up. “Yeah, I guess we should. I think we’ve had enough time in the sun today.”

They stood up and put their clothes back on and gathered up their other belongings too.

As they approached their rooms they could see Lenore and Mick sitting out on their patio and a huge, uncovered manhole in the lawn in front of them, and a man inside it.

Lenore called out to them as they approached. “There’s no water.”

Sofia thought, "Damn! I really wanted an early shower so that I could spend more time with Ted this evening."

They walked past the man in the big manhole who was bending over so they couldn't see what he was doing.

As they stepped up onto Lenore and Mick's patio, Sofia saw that they were drinking white wine as each had a glass in front of them.

Ted asked Mick, "What's happened to the water?"

Mick threw his hands in the air. "No idea. Tried asking him," he said, nodding his head towards the manhole, "but he doesn't speak a word of English. But I can tell you that he's been trying to fix it for at least 30 minutes which is when we got here.

"So get a couple of glasses and join us if you want because there's not much else to do except drink. Hopefully we won't be drinking for too long before we all get to have showers."

Ted went to his room while Sofia sat down at the table.

Lenore smiled at her and said, "Never mind. I'm sure that between the four of us we've got enough alcohol to last until we have water again. And if not, the shop's got plenty more and it's not that far away."

Ted appeared again with two wine glasses, a chilled bottle of white wine and a large bag of potato chips. "Will this do?" He asked, smiling.

Mick laughed. "You're the man."

Lenore took the wine and the glasses inside while Ted sat down and opened the bag of chips, took out a handful and offered the bag to Sofia. She too took out a handful and offered the bag to Mick who did the same and put the bag in the middle of the table.

Lenore came out with two glasses of wine, placed them in front of Ted and Sofia and went back inside for salted peanuts which she brought out in a big bowl.

Ted reached for some straight away. "Damn, I wish we could get big bags of nuts back home like you can here."

Mick said, "It's funny isn't it, that so much fruit grows here and just about every house has a garden full of fruit trees and vegetables growing, and yet the local shop is stocked with junk food like potato chips and salted nuts."

Sofia smiled. "Maybe it's because they can't grow junk food."

"Or maybe," said Mick mischievously, "it's not junk food. It's seeds and if you plant them, fruit and vegetables grow. It's just us ignorant foreigners who think it's food."

Ted lifted one eyebrow. "Just how many glasses have you had so far?"

Lenore laughed and patted Mick's arm. "Ignore him. He's just in a silly mood."

Mick patted Lenore's hand on his arm and winked at her affectionately.

Sofia picked up her glass and took a sip of her wine to stop herself looking at Lenore and Mick so that they wouldn't see the complete look of surprise on her face at how affectionate they were with each other. The last time they'd all sat and had a drink together, the two of them had seemed to be at war with each other. What a difference a few days had made. But it was a good difference.

Ted suddenly voiced what she was thinking. "Wow! You two seem much happier now then you were last time we all sat here."

Mick and Lenore smiled at each other then Mick said, "Yeah. I've come to realise she's not such a bad old bird after all."

Lenore added, "And I decided that I can put up with this old guy for a few more years yet."

"Great," said Ted. "Then we'll stay for another drink if the water still isn't on by the time we finish this one."

As it turned out, it was two hours before it was back on, by which time the four of them had laughed a lot, drank a couple more drinks and eaten every packet of junk food they had between them.

Sofia had been trying to drink slowly and had also drank a couple of glasses of water. But it wasn't easy to restrict herself because they were all having such a good time and it was all too easy to go with the flow of happy vibes. And her face ached with laughter at all the funny things that were said.

Eventually Lenore said, "I shouldn't have eaten all that. It's so fattening."

"Now, now," said Mick. "You're a glutton so just admit it and stop trying to hide it."

Lenore feigned annoyance at him. "I'm not a glutton. I just usually stay away from too much high-fat food."

Mick leaned towards Sofia and Ted. "I've told her before, she shouldn't try and run away from her problems. Unless of course she's fat, and then running is good for her."

They all laughed and Lenore play-slapped him on the shoulder, and said, "Hey look. The manhole's covered. The water must be back on."

They all turned and looked at the manhole cover that was now back in place.

Mick said, "OK, how's this for a plan. We all go and have showers, I'll order a couple of takeaway pizzas and we'll all meet back here."

They all nodded and Ted said, "seems like a plan."

Lenore and Mick stood up and headed inside while Sofia and Ted briefly kissed then headed to their own rooms.

As Sofia reached her door, she got her key out of her tote bag and let herself into her room, closing the patio door and curtains behind her.

She switched on the light and looked around. This little room looked and smelled so familiar to her that it felt like home.

It saddened her that she'd be leaving in three days. Only three days! She didn't want this life in Corfu to end.

But she knew it would.

For now though, she'd make the most of the time left here and enjoy every single minute.

Starting right now with heading for the shower so that they could all continue their most unexpected, yet most enjoyable evening together.

Chapter 16

Tuesday to Thursday. Days 12 to 14

To Sofia, it seemed like the next three days flew by much more quickly than the rest, yet at the same time, she and Ted seemed to spend more time together than ever before.

They held hands a lot, laughed a lot, were extremely intimate, ate all their meals together and slept together every night.

Their days were spent swimming, walking, eating and talking. And they talked a lot.

They discussed their families, past relationships and present living and working habits.

But they never mentioned Jason.

They did however, talk about seeing each other once they got home and decided it was Ted who would come and stay with Sofia on the weekend after they returned home which would give each of them a chance to catch up on their work. Sofia had a wedding dress to finish and had planned on doing most of the hand-beading on the bodice while she was in Corfu, but had done very little during her holiday.

In her mind she had imagined that she would spend her time here with ample opportunity to get her work done, plus swim in the pool, walk on the beach and sit and read at the local bars.

But it hadn't been like that at all. Instead she'd spent nearly all her time with Ted and Lenore and Mick.

She'd also thought that by the end of her two-week break, she'd be eager to go home and back to her usual life, minus Jason.

But instead she wanted to stay in her new home in Corfu.

The sound of Ted's voice brought her out of her reverie. But she didn't hear what he said. "What?"

She and Ted were sitting and having drinks with Lenore and Mick on their patio, which seemed to be a regular thing.

Ted continued. "Lenore said we should all go out for a meal together seeing it's our last night."

It felt so strange to think that they'd all be leaving in the morning. She tried to look happy. "Sounds like a plan. Where are we going?"

Lenore said, "I thought about that big restaurant at the end of the lane on the left-hand side of the road. It's got plenty of covered outdoor tables out the back, and a pretty decent menu."

Ted looked at Sofia. "I don't think we've been to that one yet, have we?"

"Yeah, but we only sat on the veranda at the front for a drink."

Lenore held up her palm towards them. "Trust me. We've been there a couple of times and the food's good and the tables are spread out enough so that they're not all cramped up together like they are at the restaurant here on site. I hate it when they squeeze tables in like that."

Mick agreed. "Yeah, me too. But that big restaurant at the end of the street isn't posh but it is comfortable and the food portions are huge. So it's 4.30 now," he continued, "so how about if we finish our drinks, get ready and all meet back here at 7 o'clock. That way we've got plenty of time to get some packing done too."

Sofia felt a twinge of sadness at the mention of their impending departure. It all just felt so final as though they'd never see each other again. Or maybe it was that she was enjoying being there so much that she just didn't want it to end.

Ted said, "I've finished my drink already," and nodded towards his empty beer bottle on the table to prove it.

Mick glanced at the small amount of wine still in Lenore and Sofia's glasses and at the mouthful of beer in his own bottle and said, "OK Speedy. We're not that far behind you."

As he spoke he picked up his bottle and drank the last of his beer.

Sofia and Lenore picked up their glasses, drank their remaining wine and placed their glasses back on the table in almost one synchronised movement.

"Well," said Lenore with a deep sigh, "that's it then. That's the last time we'll sit here in the afternoon and drink together." She looked out wistfully across the garden and said, "I'm going to miss this old place."

Mick patted her thigh. "Yeah, but we've got plenty more places to sit and have afternoon drinks. We've only just started our world tour."

Lenore turned to look at him and put her palm across the back of his neck. "but this one has special memories."

Mick rubbed her thigh and smiled. "Good memories that we can take with us and enjoy."

Lenore leaned in and kissed him and smiled. "You bet."

Ted interrupted them. "Well if you two young lovebirds have finished, it's time we all went to pack and get ready for dinner."

Sofia stood up. "I'm going for a shower."

Ted stood up too and they stepped off the patio. He kissed her briefly and said, "See you back here at seven."

Mick, who was already collecting the bottles and glasses from the table, waved a hand towards them and turned to go inside.

Sofia turned and left too.

Inside, her own room seemed somewhat depressing yet at the same time she felt like she wanted to stay there forever.

She sighed and started opening all the drawers in the room and taking out all the contents that were hers and placed them all on the bed.

Then she removed all her clothes from the wardrobe and placed them on the bed too.

She stood back and looked at it all and then removed all the items she still needed like an outfit for that night and for travelling plus her hair dryer and brush and comb.

She then scanned the rest of the items to see if she'd missed anything.

The things she'd need for travelling home, like her passport and plane tickets, she put in her small backpack that she'd be taking on the plane with her again.

One of the things she picked up was her cell phone which she hadn't used because she'd had it turned off the whole time.

She turned her phone on. The battery was still 50% charged.

There were several unread text messages. Some were from her friends but most were from Jason. She scrolled through them. The earlier ones were saying how much he was missing her. The later ones seemed frantic. He was asking why she wasn't responding or answering his calls.

She looked at her call log. There were a couple of missed calls from friends and ten from Jason. He'd also left voicemails but she didn't want to listen to them.

But she thought she should at least assure him that she was alright.

So she sent a short text message. "My phone has been switched off. Didn't C yr messages or calls till now. Had a gr8 time. See you soon." But even as she typed the words and hit "send" she knew that she didn't want to see him soon. Or at any time.

She picked up her phone charger and an English-to-Greek plug adapter that she'd been using with her hair dryer and began to plug them in together. But before she could finish, her phone rang and from the caller ID she saw it was Jason.

She accepted the call. "Hi."

Jason's familiar, yet almost forgotten voice came through the phone. "Finally! I've been going out of my mind with worry! Why didn't you answer my calls?" He sounded angry, but she felt that she didn't want to put up with any more of his drama.

Without any emotion she asked, "Didn't you read my text?"

"Of course I did but I don't believe it! No one goes on holiday and turns their phone off the whole time."

"I told you I was going to before I left, remember?"

"Yeah, I do. But I didn't think you would. Turning your phone off for so long is crazy!"

Sofia didn't respond, so Jason asked, "Are you still there?"

"Yeah." But what she really wanted to do was hang up.

"What's the matter?" He asked angrily.

"I've been here for two weeks having a wonderful time and now you call me and start yelling. Just calm down or I'm going to turn my phone off again right now."

Jason spoke more calmly but she could tell he was still angry. "I'm sorry, all right? It's just that I was worried and it's not been the same without you here. I've missed you in every way imaginable. Especially in bed. It's no fun sleeping alone every night without your hot little body beside me."

Ugh! She hated his assumption that they were still a couple. "Jason you're unbelievable. Do you remember why I left? It was to put some distance between us so that we could think about whether or not to stay together, and I've been giving it A LOT of thought."

Jason took a couple of seconds to respond. "And what have you thought? Look Sofia, all I know is that I've been missing you like crazy and I can't wait to see you again."

"It sounds more like you're missing sex, not me."

He started sounding annoyed again. "For God's sake! Stop reading things into everything I say. I said I missed you, not just in bed."

Suddenly there was a knock on Sofia's door which was open, so she held the phone away from her face and said, "Come in."

Amy stepped into the room. "Hi. I saw you come back to your room." Then she saw the phone in Sofia's hand. "Oh sorry. I'll come back."

"No, no. It's fine," Sofia said, motioning her to sit on the bed. Amy sat on the opposite side to Sofia.

To Jason Sofia said, "Look, I have to go. I'm in the middle of packing and my phone doesn't have much charge so it'll probably cut out soon anyway."

"Who's your visitor?"

"It's a neighbour. Look, I've got to go Jason."

Amy's eyebrows arched up when Sofia said his name.

Jason sounded furious when he spoke. "Oh, I see. You're having such great time with all your new friends that you're too busy to speak to me now."

As he spoke Sofia tapped "Speaker" on her phone and put it on the bed on top of the pile of her belongings so that Amy could hear both sides of the conversation.

To Jason she said, "I don't know why you're so angry. I told you I'd turn off my phone while I was here, you panicked when you couldn't reach me so I texted you to say I'm OK and now you're mad at me."

Jason ignored what she said. "So how many other little friends have you met while you've been there and how many are guys?"

Amy grinned and put a hand over her mouth as though stifling a laugh.

Sofia said, "Well strangely enough, it's not an all-female island. Just yesterday a male waiter served me in a restaurant."

"And who were you with at the restaurant?" He was clearly fuming.

Sofia smiled at Amy and shook her head. "Look Jason, I haven't got the time or patience right now. But one thing I can tell you is that after talking to you today, I don't need to think about our relationship anymore."

Jason started to speak but she cut him off. "No! You listen for a change. I've been here for two whole weeks without your unnecessary drama and it's been wonderful. I didn't realise how much I hated all your childish bullshit until I was away from it for a while.

"But what I do know is that I won't put up with it any more. Never! Do you understand?

"I'm going out to dinner with friends tonight and I need to get ready so I'm going to hang up now and turn my phone off so don't call me because I won't answer.

"We'll talk when I get back, but there's going to be changes." And then she pressed "End Call."

Amy was grinning from ear to ear. "That was good. Glad I didn't miss it. You're right about his childish attitude. How do you put up with that?"

"I don't anymore. As soon as I get home I'm dumping him."

"So you're not going to give him a chance to change?"

Sofia plugged her phone into the socket next to the bed and it started charging. "People never change. We are who we are. He's always sorry and behaves really well whenever he's worried I'm going to end things with him, but he can't keep pretending for long so he soon lapses back into his usual pettiness."

"So why have you stayed with him so long?"

"Because I was happy being single and so was he. It's much easier to be with one person who doesn't want to live with me rather than date other men who ALWAYS want to live with me eventually."

"So is it Ted who's made you change your mind? Are you going to see him when you get home? Do tell." Amy grinned as she spoke.

"Yeah, he's coming to my place next weekend. We both need a week to catch up with things like work and then he's coming to Bath for a couple of nights."

"Oooh!" Said Amy, clapping her hands together. "It sounds great. You're so lucky to have met him. I've seen the two of you around the place almost every day and you look so happy together."

"What about you? How's it going with your relationship?"

Amy shrugged. "Oh, that's definitely over. As soon as we get home I'm leaving him. I'll wait till he goes to work on Monday and pack my things and go. I'll leave him a note, but I don't think he'll really care that I've gone."

"Where will you go?"

"I can go and stay with my sister for a while until I can find a place of my own. I'm going to talk to her this weekend, but I'm sure she won't mind. I've stayed with her before."

"It's strange isn't it how this holiday has put an end to both our relationships. I just wish yours was for a happy reason too."

"Oh it is," said Amy smiling. "I'd much rather be alone than be with him any longer. This is going to be a fresh start for me. I'm thinking of moving away and starting a new job. I also might study part-time for a degree so that I can have a proper career and earn decent money for a change."

"Wow. You've really given this a lot of thought."

"You betcha. I've had so much time to think while I've been here and I've decided to do it right. I'm going to sort out my life so that I'm independent, both emotionally and financially. That way I'm in control and if I meet someone else one day, fine. If I don't? Fine. Either way is OK because I won't need them. And I won't make the mistake of living with anyone again. I'm either married or single. No more of this in-between living together, just like you did."

Sofia was amazed and pleased at Amy's independent resolve. "Good for you. I have to say that not living with Jason, or anyone, was one of my smarter decisions. It's better to wait until you meet your soul mate.

"Speaking of which, I have to get packed and start getting ready to go out. We're having a last meal together with our neighbours tonight."

"Yeah, I've noticed the four of you getting pretty chummy lately."

"They're all right. I'll miss hanging out with them."

"Well," said Amy, jumping to her feet, "I'll love you and leave you so that you can get ready. And I wish you all the best in your future Mrs Ted life."

Sofia stood up and moved around to the front of the small couch at the bottom of the bed. Amy moved too and stood facing her.

The two women embraced warmly. As they pulled apart Sofia held Amy's hands in hers. "I hope it all works out well for you. I'm so glad we met."

Amy squeezed Sofia's hands. "Me too. And don't worry about me. I'll be fine. I'll be great. There's no stopping me now." She briefly hugged Sofia again and said, "Bye," before turning and quickly leaving without looking back.

Sofia felt Amy's sadness at saying goodbye for the last time and tears welled in her eyes as she watched her go. She would miss her and it felt strange to be saying a final goodbye.

But now she had things to do. She started folding all her clothes and putting them in her suitcase along with her other belongings. Then she showered and changed, putting on a pair of plain knee-length shorts and a loose, tie-dyed cotton top. It was a warm night so she didn't want to wear anything clingy.

Next she blow-dried her hair and brushed it through. Then she put what she needed in her handbag and headed off to meet up with the others.

The restaurant they went to had a large, rear outdoor area where they sat at a table big enough for eight.

There weren't many other people there so no one was seated near them which Sofia thought was just as well because they ended up laughing and talking loudly the whole time.

Everyone seemed to be in high spirits which she thought might be because it was their last night so they all wanted to make sure they enjoyed it.

Back at their rooms after dinner they decided to get out all their remaining alcohol and drink it.

They all separated and went to their own kitchens to get what they had.

When they put it all on Lenore and Mick's patio table it amounted to 6 small bottles of beer and half a bottle of white wine.

Mick perused the small collection of bottles and said, "Hmm..meagre pickings."

Sofia agreed. "Yes but we don't want to drink too much if we're all travelling tomorrow."

Mick laughed. "And we want to be up on time too. We're being picked up at six in the morning. How about you?"

Ted said, "Ten thirty for us so we can sleep in a bit."

"You lucky bastards," said Mick and they all laughed and sat down. "I'll tell you what," he continued. "How about if we each have a beer and then me and Ted will have another while you girls finish the wine."

Lenore grabbed a beer and twisted off the top. "Done." She said, slamming the bottle top on the table. She raised her bottle. "Here's to moving on tomorrow."

The other three each opened a bottle and raised it to clink with Lenore's.

"Cheers," they all said in unison.

Tomorrow! Sofia was struck by the word because she still found it hard to believe that they were leaving so soon. Or leaving at all.

Later, when they'd finished their drinks and swapped contact details with Lenore and Mick, she and Ted went back to her room and slept embraced in each other's arms.

And as Sofia drifted off to sleep, she again felt that there was nowhere else on earth she'd rather be right now. And she dreaded waking up there in the morning for the last time.

Chapter 17

Friday. Day 15

It seemed so strange to be leaving. It felt sad when she put on her backpack and wheeled her suitcase out onto the patio, locking the door for the last time and leaving behind a room that had felt like home but was now void of all her belongings.

She and Ted walked to the reception desk together where they handed in their keys and waited for the bus to take them to the airport.

As they waited, many people passed them. Some were waiting to go on a day trip, some were headed for the bar, while others were clearly heading for a day at the beach or the pool. So many strangers looking forward to a relaxing day, while she and Ted had to leave. It didn't seem fair.

Soon their bus arrived and once their suitcases were stowed on board, they chose a seat together and the bus departed. Within minutes, they drove out of the resort and were headed to the first of several more where other passengers were to be collected.

Because they'd already taken this journey when they arrived, they knew it would take two hours. But they had plenty of time because their plane wasn't due to leave until 3.30pm so they could have lunch at the airport.

As Sofia looked out of the window, she tried to implant an image of the scenery in her mind so that she could recall it later with fond memories.

Music was playing on the bus in the background, which was pleasant.

She and Ted were holding hands the whole time and she felt him squeeze hers. She turned to look at him and he gave her a sad smile. "Don't worry. We'll see each other again next week. It won't be long."

She appreciated his attempt to cheer her up. "I know. But it's been so great being here. I just don't want it to end."

"But it has to end so that it can get better. You'll see."

Just then the song that was playing ended and another began. It was the band called No Doubt singing their sad, yet popular song, "Don't Speak" which somehow echoed Sofia's mood.

The lyrics that Gwen Stefani was singing had never sounded so poignant as they did right then. "You and me, we used to be together, every day together, always..."

Sofia felt like her heart was breaking as the song continued with, "With my head in my hands I sit and cry...You and me, I can see us dying, are we?"

To Ted she said, "I wish they'd play a different song because this one is killing me."

Ted smiled. "I was just thinking the same thing. You'd think they'd play more uplifting songs on a long journey."

Sofia smiled at Ted. "But unlike in the song, we're not ending, right? We're just beginning."

"Absolutely," he said and kissed her.

She squeezed his hand and realised that instead of feeling down and anxious about leaving, she should be making the most of the last few hours they still had together here. So she changed the subject. "It's such a different landscape here isn't it?" She said, looking out the window. "Every single thing is different from back home; the buildings, the people, even the dirt looks a different colour."

Ted rested his chin on her shoulder as he too looked out of the window and said,"Yeah, and it's good different. I've enjoyed the different culture and way of life here. Much more laid back than old London."

Sofia agreed. "I don't think you could get much different than between London and Corfu. For a start, London doesn't have a beach."

Ted gave a short laugh. "And Corfu doesn't have underground tube stations or a royal palace."

"It will seem strange to be back home. I feel like we've been here so long."

Ted put his arms around her. "Best holiday ever, I reckon, and it's not over yet."

Sofia loved the way he always seemed to say exactly what she wanted to hear.

The bus continued to stop and fill up with more passengers as Sofia and Ted continued to embrace and talk about how much they liked Corfu.

Eventually, they arrived at the airport and they had to wait the longest to get their suitcases because they'd been stowed first so were at the back of the luggage compartment under the bus. But they didn't mind the wait because they had nowhere else to be.

Once inside the airport they saw that the check-in desk for their flight was already open so they gratefully got their boarding passes and handed over their suitcases. They were then free to look around the airport.

In the book store, they each bought a book to read on the journey home. Sofia bought a novel and Ted bought a book about computer coding. She was surprised such a book was available at the airport, thinking that most people would be looking for a light read.

Then they went to a cafe and had coffee and cake, deciding not to have a full meal because they would probably be served food on the plane.

Sofia looked at her surroundings. "It's a bit different to where we had breakfast."

They'd ventured out a couple of hours before their bus arrived to have breakfast at their favourite local cafe.

It had been a warm, sunny morning so they'd sat at a table on the veranda to enjoy the view there just one last time.

Their surroundings at the airport seemed so closed in and sterile with a constant loud hum from the chatter of so many people.

Ted looked around and said, "Well, this place isn't great but the company still is." He winked at her as he said it.

Sofia laughed. "That is so corny."

Ted smiled at her. "Yeah, but you'd better get used to it."

Sofia put her hand on his arm and said with a smile, "Just remember that I love you despite all your corny lines not because of them."

Ted grinned cheekily and said, "Yeah, but it always gets me da goils."

Sofia grinned back. "But I would have thought you wanted women not girls."

"Goils is goils."

"Just when I thought you couldn't get any cornier..." And they both laughed together.

They stayed at the cafe sipping their coffee and chatting until they heard the announcement that their flight was boarding, so they went to join the queue and get on board.

Their seats on the plane were near the back and Sofia took the seat by the window. Ted sat next to her and to their relief, no one sat in the third seat next to the aisle.

The flight was three hours, but it didn't seem that long. They spent the entire time discussing what they were going to do when they saw each other again.

Sofia said that she would make a dinner reservation for them at a local restaurant the following weekend.

Ted would arrive late next Friday afternoon and Sofia would meet him at the train station. They wanted to spend a quiet evening together at Sofia's house and the next day, she would take him on a tour of the city and then they'd go out for dinner.

It all sounded so great and Sofia was looking forward to it, but knew that it might seem so different to being with him in Corfu.

Soon came the announcement that the plane was about to start it's descent to Heathrow Airport so they all had to adjust their watches back to English time and put on their seatbelts.

Sofia felt butterflies in her stomach and it wasn't from the descent. It was from the thought of saying goodbye to Ted and stepping back into her normal life.

Once the plane landed they went through the usual hustle and bustle of getting off the plane and collecting their luggage. It seemed chilly compared to Corfu

Then they went to look at train times because that was the next leg of their journey home.

Sofia saw that her train was due in 20 minutes and she still had to get downstairs to the station, so it was time to say goodbye to Ted.

They embraced and he kissed her on the lips. It was a brief goodbye for which Sofia was somewhat grateful.

Ted said, "Don't worry, we'll be back together soon."

"I know. It just seems so weird to be leaving you after all this time. But I've got to go. Don't want to miss my train."

"I'll walk you to the station."

"No don't. It's better if I just go. You've got your own train to catch."

"OK. I'll give you a call tomorrow night. That'll give us both time to recover and catch up with doing the laundry." They both gave a small laugh because it was true. They each had a suitcase full of dirty clothes. It just seemed like such an all-too-common thing to mention.

"Talk to you soon." Sofia grabbed the handle of her suitcase and headed for the train station without looking back.

The journey back to Bath seemed so solitary after being with other people constantly for the past two weeks. It was early evening and most people getting on and off the train were merely coming home from after a day at work. Others were dressed up and heading for a night out.

Sofia felt mentally exhausted and couldn't wait to get home.

When the train arrived in Bath, she stepped off and walked home. She could have caught a cab but she wanted to walk, even though she'd have to wheel her suitcase the whole way and it felt a bit chilly. As she walked she thought how strange it felt to be home. She'd lived here for years, yet after just two weeks away it seemed somewhat foreign while at the same time familiar.

It was 30 minutes before she arrived at her door. She retrieved her keys from her backpack, unlocked the door, switched on the hallway light, and stepped inside, wheeling her suitcase behind her.

The house smelled a little musty from being closed up for so long and while it was sad to be away from Ted, it felt comfortable to be back in her own home again.

First things first, she left her bags in the hallway, turned on the heating, and then went straight to the kitchen to make a cup of coffee. Once it was ready she took it into the living room and sipped it while sitting on the couch. She immediately felt her body relaxing, even though she hadn't realised she'd been tense.

She sat there for 20 minutes savouring every mouthful of the warm drink. She reached for her phone which she'd put on the coffee table when she sat down, and turned it on. Thankfully there were no missed calls or text messages from Jason.

She put the phone back on the coffee table and relaxed back with her warm drink. She shouldn't have to face Jason until tomorrow so she'd enjoy her evening without him.

Once she'd finished her coffee it was time to tackle the luggage.

She put her empty coffee cup in the kitchen sink and took her bags through the kitchen and into the laundry room.

Her dirty clothes still smelled of Corfu. She took them all out one by one and sorted them into separate piles on the floor; delicates, light colours and dark colours. She put the pile of dark colours into the washing machine along with the soap powder and fabric softener and set the timer so that they would be washed early in the morning and would be ready by the time she'd had breakfast.

Then she went upstairs to put all her other things away before coming back down to shake all the sand from her suitcase outside the back door before stowing it away in the cupboard under the stairs.

Now for a shower. The hot water felt good and she stayed there for a few extra minutes to feel the therapeutic effect washing all over her.

Once she was clean and her hair was washed she reluctantly turned off the water and stepped out of the shower to dry herself.

She went into the bedroom and dressed in a cotton nightgown and robe and dried her hair.

Then she went back downstairs to make herself something to eat. She didn't feel like cooking so she decided to just throw a few oven chips and a pie in the oven. While they were cooking she switched on the TV and started scanning through the channels to see what was on.

Suddenly her phone rang. With dread she looked at the caller ID and saw that it was Jason. She really didn't want to talk to him so would have to put him off.

She picked up her phone and said, "Hi."

Jason sounded happy. "Are you home yet?"

"Yeah. Just."

"Great! I'll be there soon." Before she could respond he hung up. Damn! She really didn't want to see him today, or any day for that matter. It was a pity he just couldn't disappear so that she didn't have to deal with him.

Within minutes there was a knock at her door. She opened it and Jason stepped straight in, put his arms around her and kissed her lips. She grimaced and pulled away from him. "For goodness sake, Jason, I'm exhausted. You could at least say hello first."

"I've just missed you so much." He grabbed her backside as he said it and then walked passed her into the living room.

She reluctantly followed. He looked at the TV and then went into the kitchen and looked at her dinner through the glass oven door.

Turning to her he seemed annoyed. "I thought you said you'd only just got back? Looks like you've showered and put dinner on so you must have been back for a while."

"Only long enough to shower and put dinner on. So what?"

"You said you'd ring me once you were home." He stepped up close to her and grabbed her around her waist, pulling her up against him. "Haven't you missed me? I've missed you." Again his hand found her backside.

She pulled away from him. "I didn't call you because I'm tired. I was just going to have something to eat and go to bed."

"Bed sounds good to me."

"I meant alone. Damn it Jason! I'm just tired. I didn't call you because I didn't want to have this conversation with you. Why don't you come round tomorrow and we'll talk then."

He again made a grab for her but she pushed him away. "Just stop it will you! Why do you never listen to what I say?"

Jason got annoyed. "I just want to be with you is that so wrong? I haven't seen you for two weeks."

Now Sofia was annoyed too. "No you don't want to be with me. You just want to have sex and that's not the same. If you give a damn about me, you'll leave this till tomorrow."

"Boy you've come back in a bad mood."

"Just go! I'm exhausted."

Jason headed towards the door. "Fine. I'll see you tomorrow when you're in a better mood." Sofia didn't care what he said just as long as he went. She didn't want to have the dreaded conversation with him tonight. She just wanted him to leave because she found his touch disgusting.

He slammed the door on his way out. Sofia quickly followed him and locked it, just to make sure he couldn't walk back in. With relief, she heard his car door slam, the engine start and drive away.

She walked back into the living room, grateful to be alone again but she now felt on edge, so she went to the fridge and took out a bottle of white wine and poured herself a glass. She took a sip and carried the glass to the coffee table in front of the couch. Then she got out a knife and fork and put them on the table too.

When her food was ready she sat down and enjoyed her meal with the glass of wine while she watched a comedy show on TV. Soon she felt relaxed again and so went back for another glass of wine.

Eventually she felt herself getting sleepy so she turned off the TV, put her glass and dishes in the kitchen sink, and headed off to bed, turning out the lights as she went.

It felt good to be back home and in her own bed which was far more comfortable than the bed in her room in Corfu.

The only thing that niggled at her was having to see Jason tomorrow and tell him that she didn't want to see him anymore. It wasn't telling him that was going to be the problem, but getting him to understand that she meant it.

Well, for now she'd forget about it and worry about it tomorrow because as Scarlet said so famously in the movie Gone With The Wind, "I'll think about that tomorrow, because after all, tomorrow is another day."

And with that comforting thought, she drifted off to sleep.

Chapter 18

Saturday

Sofia opened her eyes the next morning to a bright and sunny day. She'd forgotten to set her alarm clock the night before and was surprised to see that she'd slept in and it was now after 9am. She must have been more tired than she realised.

After getting ready she went downstairs and saw that the washing machine had finished the early cycle she'd set it for the previous evening, so she hung the clothes out and put some more in to wash.

Then it was time for a leisurely breakfast and afterwards she washed the dishes, some of which were from her dinner the previous evening. By this time the washing machine had finished again so she hung the clothes out on the washing line and put another load in the machine. Boy, she was getting through things breezily today, which was good because she had a lot of sewing to catch up on since she did so little on holiday.

She got out her bag of work and looked at the beading she'd already done. Then she turned on the TV and put a DVD into the player so that she could watch a few episodes of one of her favourite shows while she worked.

She sat for several hours getting plenty done and stopping a couple of times for coffee and lunch.

Then in the middle of the afternoon, she heard the sound she'd been dreading. It was a knock at the door which probably meant that Jason was there. She paused her DVD before getting up to answer it.

He strode past her as soon as she opened the door. "So...are you in a better mood this morning?"

Sofia sighed heavily and followed him into the living room. "Is that really all you have to say to me? Not hello, or how was your holiday or I'm sorry for acting like such an arsehole last night?"

Jason's brow wrinkled. "What the hell is wrong with you? Last night you were mad at me and today you're still mad at me. What is your problem?"

Sofia decided that now was as good a time as any to tell him that their relationship was over. "I don't have a problem. I've just spent two weeks with people who liked me and I liked them. And we all got along and had a great time. I had a ball while I was away.

"I spent the whole time laughing and smiling with no drama whatsoever. And now as soon as I see you it's back to arguing again."

Jason cut her off. "Fine. Fine. You made a few friends and now you want me to act sweetly. But look at it from my point of view. I've been missing you so much and as soon as I touched you last night you acted like I had rabies or something. For God's sake Sofia, you were gone for a long time and I missed you."

He put his hand on her upper arm and tried to pull her towards him. She pulled her arm out of his grasp. "Just don't!"

"See? You're doing it again. And don't say that I only want sex."

"Well don't you?"

"Of course I WANT it. I haven't had it for two weeks."

"I haven't had sex with you for two weeks either, but I'm not grabbing at you." She hoped he wouldn't notice her use of the extra words "with you" because she didn't want to lie and say that she hadn't had sex for two weeks.

She continued in a softer tone. "Look Jason, I think you've forgotten why I went away in the first place. It was because we weren't getting along and so the whole idea was that I would go away and give us both some time to think about whether or not we still wanted to be together, because things couldn't go on as they were. And so far, nothing seems to have changed."

Sofia sat on the sofa and Jason sat next to her. They were facing each other with their knees almost touching. She wanted to position herself so that he couldn't make a grab for her again.

Jason looked somewhat confused. "So what do you want me to do?"

"Well I've been thinking about us and our relationship while I've been away and I assume you were thinking about it too."

"Sure I was. And all I could think about while you were gone was how much I missed you. So I want us to stay together. But listen...before we talk any more about this, can we just go upstairs for a while, because if I don't empty these soon they're going to burst." Jason put his hand between his legs as he spoke. Sofia felt sick.

"THAT is what I don't want. I don't want to be just the person who's handy for sex any time you feel like it.

"While I was away I met lots of people and got invited out for drinks and meals with them and we'd even sit together at our apartments and have drinks on the patio. And it was fun and everyone thought I was pretty amazing that I lived on my own and supported myself through my handmade wedding dress business. They were really impressed with my work when they saw me doing my sewing while I was there.

"Yet you think what I do for a living is a joke. You say it's not real work. You're always really demeaning when you talk about me and what I do."

"Oh God! Do we have to go over this again?"

"What I'm saying is that nothing has changed. You just want us to continue on as though nothing has happened. But you need to hear me and understand what I'm about to tell you."

Jason, for once, didn't say anything and seemed ready to listen to her so she continued. "I went on holiday and had a good time. I met a lot of people and I enjoyed every minute. And one thing that I realised was that I wasn't missing you. In fact it was the opposite. I was glad you weren't there or you would have spoiled it. Which means that I don't want to be with you anymore.

"And since I arrived home I've felt the same. I didn't call you last night when I got home because I didn't want to see you. And when you came round and tried to grab me, I didn't want you to touch me either.

"And even now, you're here but I don't want you to be. Not only did I not miss you, I felt relieved to be away from you, and that's not how it's supposed to be. And all you want is sex. But I don't. Not with you, anyway."

Jason's face suddenly changed. He quickly stood up and he fixed her with a really angry stare. She'd never seen him look like that before. She stood up too and took a step back as he started to speak.

"Not with me? You don't want to have sex...with me? Then who do you want to have it with?"

Before she could answer he began to yell at her.

"You've been sleeping with someone else. HAVEN'T YOU!"

He was really angry so Sofia stayed quiet, hoping that if she didn't say anything, he'd leave sooner.

"I'm right, aren't I? You didn't go there and just meet a lot of people. You slept with them. Didn't you?"

She still said nothing.

"You went there and opened your legs like a dirty slut. Can you deny it?"

Sofia continued to stare at him expressionless, willing him to just leave.

"Well maybe us splitting up isn't your choice anymore. You've been talking down to me so much lately and accusing me of being a rotten bastard for not treating you properly

"And all the time you've been acting like a sneaky, little whore behind my back."

His expression suddenly changed from angry to unsure.

"How long have you been doing this? Have you been having sex with other guys all along? Before you even went on your slutty holiday?"

Still she said nothing.

"You have, haven't you? That's why you can't deny it."

Then he looked smug as well as angry again. "I've found you out, haven't I? I bet you've been making a fool of me all along while at the same time you pretend to be so righteous and indignant if you didn't think I was treating you nicely enough.

"Well I don't want to be with a slut like you. You don't get to tell me how I should treat you anymore, because I'm going to treat you with the contempt you deserve."

Jason took a step towards her so that they were almost touching and raised his hand and pointed his finger at her face. "You disgust me! You know that? All this time you've been talking down to me to try and make me believe that I'm the bad one in this relationship, when all along it was you."

For a split second Sofia was scared he was going to hit her. But instead he turned and walked towards the front door as he continued to yell.

"Well you don't get to tell me to go away because I don't want anything to do with a SLUT like you. Just stay away from me. I deserve better than a whore like you!"

And with that, he slammed the door and was gone.

Sofia quickly went to the door and locked it, just in case he thought about coming back in to yell some more.

While he'd been shouting at her she hadn't spoken because she didn't care what he thought of her, she just wanted him gone. So the fact that he thought she'd been unfaithful to him the whole time they'd been together, worked in her favour because now he'd given himself a reason to not want to be with her.

And as long as he thought badly of her, he wouldn't want to come back. She knew that he wouldn't want to lose face by ever being with her again, which was what she wanted.

Even if things didn't work out with Ted, she still wouldn't want to be with Jason anymore. She hadn't lied to him when she said she hadn't missed him one bit.

Later, around 7 pm, Ted phoned. It was so good to hear his voice. They talked for over 2 hours. Sofia told him about the breakup and said that Jason had taken it really well. She didn't want to tell him all the terrible things Jason had accused her of, so she just kept it simple.

Ted had some news of his own. He said that he'd spoken to his ex-wife and put his foot down about her bad behaviour towards him. He'd told her that he could afford the best lawyer and that she was to speak civilly to him from now on and stop blocking his efforts to sell their previous joint home. To his surprise, she backed down and agreed to be reasonable about everything and even half apologised for her previous behaviour.

Sofia said, "That's wonderful. What made you do that?"

"I got the idea from you and what you said to Mick. He was being pushed around and belittled by Lenore, but once he stood up to her and read her the riot act, she backed off completely. So I thought I'd give it a go. And it worked!" He sounded surprised as well as pleased.

"Good for you."

"And now that we've got other people sorted out, how about us?"

"I can't wait to see you again."

"Me too. I've been catching up on work all day. Bet you've been doing the same."

"Yeah. I'm really behind, but I got quite a bit done today despite the fact that I forgot to set my alarm and didn't get up till after 9 o'clock. I'm not even sure how I slept so long because I went to bed early enough."

"I slept in too, and I slept deeply. I think we were both just exhausted. We had spent the whole day travelling."

"True. So are you still coming to see me?"

"I was thinking I'll still come over on the train next Friday. But I have to go into the office that day so I'll come straight after that which means I'll be in Bath at 8pm. Can you meet me at the train station?"

"I can't wait. I'll make us something to eat at my place and get it ready before you arrive."

"Sounds great. What are we going to do for the rest of the weekend?"

"We can go out on Saturday and I'll show you around. We have some amazing markets here every weekend. And I'll make a dinner reservation for Saturday night."

"I've never been to Bath before so it will be interesting. You can give me the complete guided tour."

Although she felt excited about seeing him there was still that niggling worry that things wouldn't be the same now that they were back home.

Hopefully, it would be just as good seeing him again as it was for those two weeks in Corfu.

Chapter 19

Friday

Ted and Sofia talked on the phone every night. On Thursday night he said, "See you tomorrow." She felt butterflies in her stomach when he said it. How could she be so nervous about seeing someone that she'd just spent an extremely intimate two weeks with?

But this was different. It was the test as to whether they'd still feel the same about each other now that life was about to get in the way.

Thankfully Jason hadn't bothered her all week. She had thought that he might have come around to see her, but so far so good. There had been no sign of him.

Sofia had spent the week catching up on her sewing because the dress she was working on was due for a fitting with the client soon, so she'd finished the beading on the bodice and was now sewing the whole dress together, which was always a big task with dresses such as this one that had so many beads and a lot of lace. But she didn't mind because she enjoyed sewing. She used one of her spare bedrooms as her sewing room which was completely kitted out with everything she needed including a small iron and ironing board, an overlocker on one desk and a sewing machine on another. Plus the built-in wardrobes were crammed with all her other tools of the trade plus wedding dress fabric and patterns.

Today was Friday and Ted was due in a few hours, so she spent the day cleaning and gardening just to make sure everything was perfect. She also stripped her bed and put on clean sheets. The dirty sheets she washed and put in the tumble drier so that she could fold them and put them away out of sight straight away.

Then it was time to cook. She went to the supermarket and bought everything she needed. Then it was home to make small pasties, mini pizzas, salad, coleslaw and she'd bought a couple of packets of potato chips and salted nuts to go with it, and made a chocolate cake with chocolate icing. She knew these were things that Ted would like because she'd eaten enough meals with him to know that he preferred simple food. She also put a couple of bottles of wine into the fridge to chill.

By the time she'd done everything, including the huge amount of dishes that needed washing, it was 5 o'clock. Just enough time to sit down and relax a bit before getting ready to go and meet Ted.

So she put on the TV and watched one of her favourite shows for an hour and then went upstairs to get ready. She showered and changed into a pair of cotton pants and cotton blouse. She also took a woollen shawl out of her wardrobe to wear when she went out later.

But now the bathroom looked dirty again from being used, so she went and got a spray bottle of bathroom cleaner and a dry cleaning cloth and sprayed and wiped the bathroom sink and shower. She had no idea why she felt so nervous, but she couldn't help it. She wanted everything to be perfect, not that Ted would really care how clean her house was.

Soon it was time to go. The station was only a short walk, so she wrapped her shawl around her back and upper arms, locked the door behind her and set off walking. She arrived 15 minutes early. She hadn't meant to be so off with her timing but she'd walked much faster than she'd intended and hadn't seemed able to slow down.

Once outside the station she looked at the timetable to make sure Ted's train was running on time and to see which platform it was arriving on and went inside.

Then it was time to wait. She stood in the middle of the platform because she didn't know if Ted would be sitting at the front of the train or at the back. It was a nervous wait. She was eager to see him again and felt like a school girl waiting for her 'crush' to arrive.

She stood stock still, her mind going at a hundred miles an hour without being able to concentrate on any one thought for longer than two seconds. The station was busy but she didn't notice any of it. It was as though her body was there but her mind was somewhere else.

Soon she heard the announcement that Ted's train was arriving. The butterflies in her stomach danced even harder. Within seconds she could hear the train and then it came into view. This was it. This was the moment of truth. How would they feel when they saw each other again and would they still feel the same by the end of the weekend?

Although the train was slowing down as it approached the platform, it still passed by fast enough to create a breeze that lifted her hair away from her face.

The train came to a halt with a loud squeak. There was a second or two of no activity. Then the doors began to open and passengers spilled out onto the platform.

Sofia felt so nervous and so excited at the same time as she scanned the crowds looking for his familiar face.

Then she saw him. He had already seen her and was striding towards her with a big back pack on his back and a big smile on his face. She smiled back and moved towards him. At that moment Ted had never looked so beautiful and she felt like she could cry tears of joy.

Soon their bodies collided in a tight embrace. She was so happy to see him she felt like she could hug him forever. She never wanted this feeling to go. Ted pulled away and kissed her and then hugged her again and said, "It is so good to finally be here. I was busy all week but it still seemed to drag by. You look amazing."

"Thanks. I felt the same. I've worked a lot since I got back and sometimes I had the weird feeling that being in Corfu was just a dream"

Sofia turned to leave the station. Ted took her hand and walked with her. She said, "I was so nervous waiting for you. I felt like a little school girl."

"I know exactly what you mean. I was nervous as hell as they announced that we were in Bath and would be arriving in a couple of minutes." Then he changed the subject. "This is a huge and impressive station." As they walked out of the station and onto the street he was impressed again. "Wow! Just look at his place. It's beautiful."

She smiled at him. "It's better now that you're here. It feels like I knew that you were coming, yet it seemed so surreal that you'd be here. Really weird."

"It feels the same to me too. It's as though the only place we'll ever see each other is in Corfu and being here is like two worlds colliding."

"Yeah. It is. And I'm glad you travelled light because we're walking to my place. It's not far though. Just 30 minutes or so."

"That's great. I can have a look around."

And he did. He marvelled at everything; the historic buildings, the trees, the shops - he thought it was all amazing.

Soon they arrived at Sofia's house. "Well, here we are."

Ted looked at her house and garden, slowly taking it all in. "You live here?"

Sofia felt momentarily nervous. "Yes. Why? What's wrong with it?"

Ted shook his head and laughed. "Oh God no. There's nothing wrong with it. It's great. I just imagined you lived in a tiny house but this looks like quite the mansion."

Sofia was relieved that he liked it. "Well, it's not a mansion. But it's big enough for me and my sewing business. And I like having a detached house and a garden." As she spoke they walked up the front path to the door which she unlocked and motioned for Ted to enter first."

"This is really nice," he said looking around the hallway.

Sofia stepped inside too and locked the door behind them. She went ahead of Ted into the living room. He liked everything he saw as she also showed him around the kitchen and laundry room, the front room and the two bedrooms upstairs and the bathroom.

Eventually they went into her room and she said, "You can leave your bag in here if you want."

Ted put his bag on the floor next to the bed and pulled her close. "This is what I want," and he kissed her passionately. She felt herself melt against him. This was where she wanted to be.

Their kissing became intense. Ted ran his hands up the side of her body and over her breasts. She moaned with pleasure. She ran her hands down his back and onto his tight buttocks and he let out a small moan too.

They slowly undressed each other, kissing and touching the whole time, both eager and hungry for love making.

Later, they laid naked on the bed together. Ted had his arm around her and she was snuggled up at his side.

After a few minutes he spoke. "I've missed you, you know?"

Sofia snuggled closer. "I could tell."

"Well," he laughed, "that was great. But I mean I really missed you. It seemed so strange not to be with you anymore."

"I know what you mean. I felt the same. I was nervous about seeing you again yet at the same time I was missing you like crazy."

"Yeah, I was pretty nervous too, wondering if we were crazy to think that things would be the same once we were back home and all the usual shit kicked in."

"Well, I split up with Jason and you sorted out your ex-wife so we both got rid of quite a bit of shit."

Ted laughed. "We did, didn't we? Speaking of which, have you heard from lover-boy since?"

"No. Not a thing. I thought he might have been difficult, but so far he's staying away. Maybe he could tell I meant it so there was no use trying to convince me to stay."

Sofia propped herself up on one elbow. "Anyway, enough of this talk. I've made us some food and there's a bottle of chilled wine in the fridge, so what do you say we go downstairs and have something to eat and drink?"

"Sounds like plan," said Ted, pulling his arm out from under her and sitting up on the edge of the bed. Then he turned to her and said, "It is so good to see you again."

Sofia felt so touched she could have cried. "You too," was all she could manage as she quickly turned away and started to gather up her clothes and get dressed again. She then went to the bathroom to clean herself up.

When she came back into the bedroom, Ted was already dressed and was looking in his bag. "I've brought you something," he said and took out a six-pack of Greek beer, the same one they'd been drinking on holiday.

Sofia laughed and took them from him. "Where on earth did you find them?"

"I was just looking at the beers in a local shop when I saw those. I recognised them immediately. I've never seen them here before but I probably didn't pay attention to them before we'd had them in Corfu."

They went downstairs and Ted helped her get out the food and put it on the table.

Then they cracked open a couple of beers and sat down to eat.

Sofia put the radio on so that they had some background music and they talked and laughed and ate and drank until it was late.

When they were tired, they put everything away and went upstairs to bed.

As she laid down in his arms and drifted off to sleep, she felt once again that there was nowhere else in the world she wanted to be right now. It just felt so right to be back with Ted once more.

She just hoped that they'd both feel the same by the end of the weekend.

Chapter 20

Saturday

The weekend began with a sunny morning on Saturday.

When Sofia woke up she momentarily forgot that Ted was laying beside her, but it only took a split second for her to remember and turn over to see his sweet face laying on the pillow next to hers.

She reached out and touched his face softly. "Good morning."

Ted's eyes fluttered open and he smiled at her before turning onto his back and doing a full length stretch. As his arms came back down he wrapped them around her and kissed her. "It is a good morning indeed."

"How'd you sleep?"

"Like a log. And you?"

"Ditto. Are you hungry?"

"Starving and desperate for coffee. Are we eating in or out?"

"Whichever you like. I was planning on showing you around town this morning so we can have breakfast first or have it out somewhere."

Ted laughed. "Well I have absolutely no idea what the food is like out there, but I'll happily enjoy your cooking. I'll even help you get breakfast ready."

"Sounds good to me. I'll go to the bathroom first, OK?"

"Fine by me. I want to have a shower if that's all right."

"Of course it is. You don't have to ask. I just want to have a wash and brush my teeth so I won't be long." And with that she threw back the covers and left the room. She almost wanted to skip to the bathroom because she felt so happy.

Soon they were both dressed and having breakfast. Sofia had made them vegetarian sausages and baked beans on toast, to be washed down with a glass of orange juice and two cups of coffee from her drip filter machine.

After they'd finished, Ted sat back and patted his stomach. "That was absolutely delicious."

"Thanks. I thought we should have something filling. I'll get the dishes done and we'll go out and have a look around. How about if we have lunch out because I have so much to show you."

"Sounds good to me. Have you booked us anywhere for dinner later."

"Yes. I found the perfect restaurant that only just opened the week before we went away."

"What's so perfect about it?"

"It's a Greek restaurant."

Ted was delighted. He sat back in his chair and laughed. "Wow. That is perfect. How ironic that it opened just as we were leaving for a Greek holiday."

"I know, isn't it great? We can try it out together, but I've heard that it's really popular so it might be busy."

"Doesn't matter. It will be fun."

They did the dishes together and then they left to go and explore Bath. Sofia showed him the famous Roman Bath house, Sally Lunn's bakery and tea room, The Jane Austen Centre, the Abbey, the markets, the parks and everything else she could think of.

Ted was impressed with everything he saw, especially the architecture of all the old buildings.

The day was tiring but a success.

Sofia had booked a table at the restaurant for 8pm so they went back to her house two hours earlier.

The restaurant was a 20 minute walk from Sofia's house so they had just about enough time to shower, change their clothes and for Sofia to dry her long thick, dark hair. She dressed casually in a loose, embroidered, cotton blouse and a pair of comfy pants and a jacket. Ted wore a loose, slip-on shirt and pants. Sofia thought he looked like a delightful hippy, especially with his long shaggy hair.

The restaurant was more crowded than they'd expected. All the tables were close together and all were occupied. When they entered the restaurant they were in a bar but could see the restaurant through a door on their left.

They ordered a drink at the bar and a waiter gave them each a menu. They sat at a small table while they perused the menu and placed an order. Then the waiter showed them to their table which was squashed in the middle of several others. To get to it they had to keep saying "Excuse me," as they waded through the other diners who were already eating.

They held hands across the table and talked until their meal arrived. As they ate they started to discuss their new situation now that they were back home.

Ted said, "I'm so happy to see you again. How do you feel?"

"I don't want this weekend to end. I don't want you to leave again."

"Sadly, I have to. I work from home but I do have to go into the office at the bank once a week or so. Not for the whole day. Just for meetings that I can't get out of or to show someone how to use the software that I've created for them.

"Maybe you could come and stay with me for as long as you want."

"But I wouldn't want to leave."

Ted took a moment to respond. "Then don't. Come and be with me. I have a big enough house and you can have one of the spare bedrooms for your sewing."

"I couldn't do that."

Ted looked rejected. "Why not?"

"My life is here. I have my house, my business and everyone knows me so that's how I get clients for my business because I'm so well-known."

Ted smiled a knowing smile. "You get clients because you have a unique product."

"What do you mean? There are always brides wanting dresses so I have a lot of competition from other businesses. It's a huge industry."

"Weddings may be a huge industry, but what you do is almost a one-of-a-kind. Before I met you I didn't know there was such a thing as women commissioning handmade gowns, except for the filthy rich. But you seem to make dresses that more people can afford.

"Believe me, you can take your business anywhere and it will always be popular. I'll tell you what. I'll make you a program especially for your business so that you can track everything."

Sofia smiled at him. It was so sweet how much he was trying to persuade her to live with him and even wanted to help her with her business any way he could.

But he was right that she was selling a unique service. She'd never thought about it like that before. Perhaps she could even raise her prices because all her clients were always so eager for her to design and make their dresses.

There was also no shortage of women wanting her services and she often turned them away because she always had a full schedule.

To Ted she said, "You're right. There are plenty of women wanting handmade wedding gowns. I'd just never thought about how unique my business is. But there are other things to think about."

"Like what?"

"Like living together."

"What about it?"

"Well..." Sofia wasn't sure how to phrase what she wanted to say. "I've never lived with anyone before."

"You were married before, weren't you?"

"Well, yes. But that's not my point. We were married, not just living together."

"So you want to get married? Is that what you're saying?"

"No. What I'm saying is, apart from my husband, I've never moved in with anyone and I know you're going to think this is weird, but I've never really understood why couples live together."

"I don't follow you."

She tried to explain it better. In her head, how she felt seemed simple enough, but trying to explain it to others was always difficult.

"When I split up with my husband I bought my house and have lived there alone ever since.

"Before I met Jason, I dated a couple of guys but both of them eventually wanted to move in with me. So I asked why? And in both cases they looked surprised. They saw living together as a natural progression of the relationship, but they hadn't thought past that. And I just can't see the point of doing something if there's no reason to do it. I guess you call it the 'what's in it for me?' Question.

"So I asked them both what did they exactly mean by living together? Did they mean live like housemates and share the bills and the chores? Or did they mean that they wanted to move in and that I would cook their meals and wash their clothes?

"And do you know why? When I asked them more about it, it turns out that they wanted me to cook and wash for them. That was it. There were no plans to progress the relationship any further. It seemed that they just wanted to move in and that was that. It was as though they wanted a housekeeper that they could sleep with.

"And yes, I know that most people move in together with no more plans for the future than that, but that really isn't for me. Plus London is a long way to move to just to see if we want to be together or not. Plus I'd be doing all the hard work of moving and rearranging my life and business.

"I do love you and I can't imagine my life without you now, but I just don't want to do a trial run."

Ted smiled his usual beaming smile. "Then it's the first step to getting married. We'll get engaged as soon as you move in."

"No, I wasn't hinting that I wanted you to marry me."

"I know. But you wouldn't be happy if we only cohabited, so we'll get married. Sofia, I want to spend the rest of my life with you. I want us to have children and grandchildren and grow old together. So let's start now. Let's move in together and get engaged."

"Don't you think that's a little fast?"

"Fast for what? Do you want to spend the rest of your life with me?"

"Yes I do. Very much so."

"Then why wait?"

She couldn't think of a reason. "I don't know."

"Does our being together feel wrong to you?"

"Not at all. Nothing's ever felt this right before."

"That's exactly how I feel. I was nervous as hell while I was on the train coming here, but as soon as I saw you again I knew I wanted to be with you."

Sofia put down her knife and fork, reached out and put one of her hands on Ted's. He put down his knife and fork too and held both her hands.

She said to him, "That's exactly how I felt. I was so tense while I was waiting on the platform but as soon as I saw you I was so excited and it felt so right to be with you again."

"Then let's do it."

Sofia's head was spinning with the sudden decision. "I'd have to sell my house."

"Good."

She laughed. "I'd be bringing all my stuff to your place and fitting it all in. I might have to move some of your stuff or you might have to get rid of it."

"Good. I'll sell my house too and we'll get a place of our own."

"Really? It's all just so simple to you?"

"It IS simple. You sell your house and move in with me. Then I'll sell my house and we'll buy a place of our own. In the meantime we'll buy you a ring so that our engagement will be official and as soon as we can arrange it, we'll get married. Perhaps we'll plan the wedding once we've settled into our own place because moving is hard enough without planning a wedding on top of it."

Sofia couldn't have been happier. They were staring into each other's eyes and holding hands tightly across the table. And even though the restaurant was crowded and noisy, she didn't notice anyone around them or hear what they were saying. Her attention was fixed solely on Ted, and likewise, he only had eyes for her.

Naturally, she'd eventually tell her family what her plans were and they'd think she was crazy. But she didn't care what they thought or what they said. She wanted to be with

Ted. And he was right. It was that straight forward and that simple. Nothing else mattered.

And she knew that whatever life was to throw at them in the future, together they could weather anything.

As long as they were together, nothing else would ever matter.

End.